MAGNUS
POWERMOUSE

MAGNUS POWERMOUSE

by *Dick King-Smith*

illustrated by Mary Rayner

HARPER & ROW, PUBLISHERS

Magnus Powermouse
Text copyright © 1982 by Dick King-Smith
Illustrations copyright © 1982 by Mary Rayner
All rights reserved. No part of this book may be used or reproduced in any manner whatsoever without written permission except in the case of brief quotations embodied in critical articles and reviews. Printed in the United States of America. For information address Harper & Row Junior Books, 10 East 53rd Street, New York, N.Y. 10022.
Designed by Trish Parcell
10 9 8 7 6 5 4 3 2 1
First American Edition

LIBRARY OF CONGRESS CATALOGING IN PUBLICATION DATA
King-Smith, Dick.
  Magnus Powermouse.

  Summary: A baby mouse who won't stop growing is
carried off by the ratcatcher and begins a series of
adventures.
  [1. Mice—Fiction] I. Rayner, Mary, ill. II. Title.
PZ7.K5893Mag 1984   [FIC]   83–48435
ISBN 0–06–023231–5
ISBN 0–06–023232–3 (lib. bdg.)

CONTENTS

CHAPTER I

Do Not Exceed the Stated Dose

Madeleine was a country girl. You could hear it in her speech, especially when she was excited. She carefully examined the new arrivals and then suddenly drew back, her black eyes round with surprise, her hair on end.

"Crumbs!" cried Madeleine loudly. "Just look at that great lump!" And had there been others there to look, they would have seen five normal newborn pink babies, each the size of a little fingernail, and a sixth that was newborn and pink but most definitely not normal, so huge and strong and active was it.

Already, at half an hour of age, it was beginning to crawl blindly about the nest, steamrollering its way over its brothers and sisters, and lifting its blunt snout hungrily in the air.

"Crumbs!" said Madeleine again. "He's as big as a baby rat! Whatever will his father say?"

The father of the six was a mouse of a different color. Not only had he a dark-gray coat, in contrast to Madeleine's warm brown, but he had come originally from a very different background. He had been born, in fact, behind the paneling of a room in an Oxford college, and had traveled down to Somerset as a youngster, quite by mistake, in a trunk full of

clothes. The occupant of the room had been a Professor of Classics, and with such a history of culture behind him Madeleine's husband considered himself several cuts above country mice. His name was Marcus Aurelius.

Marcus Aurelius had his own private den, close to the sitting-room fireplace. Later that day he rose from his bed of torn newspaper, where he had been reading snippets of the *Western Daily Press*. He made his way down the passage behind the sitting-room wainscot that led to the family home. This was in a hole in the wall at the back of the larder. It was the beginning of winter, and as usual they had come into the warmth of the cottage from their summer residence under the raised wooden floor of the pigsty at the bottom of the garden.

He found his wife, looking, it seemed to him, rather worried, sitting in the middle of her nest. Of babies he could see no sign.

"Well, Maddie my dear," he said, peering short-sightedly, for reading in a bad light had weakened his eyes, "when are we to hear the patter of tiny feet?"

"Oh, Markie, Markie!" cried Madeleine in a distracted voice. " 'Tisn't the patter of tiny feet we shall hear. 'Tis the thunder of hugeous big 'uns!" And she rolled upon her side to show what lay beneath her.

Marcus Aurelius gave a squeak of amazement at the sight which met his myopic eyes. Five feeble babies, already more blue than pink, fumbled weakly in search of their mother's milk; but in vain. Only too plainly it had all been drunk, by the red swollen sausage-shaped monster that lay distended in the center of the nest. And even as the horrified father watched, the giant baby bestirred itself, bullocking its way through the others and knocking them flying as it made once more for the milk bar.

At last Marcus Aurelius found his voice, after a fashion. Normally long-winded, the shock reduced him to a series of gasps.

"Never in all my . . . what on earth . . . how?" he gulped.

"Oh, Markie," said Madeleine in low tones, as though fearful that the huge infant might overhear her. "I've never seen such a big 'un neither. And it ain't a changeling, if that's what you're thinking, it's mine all right, I should know. And as for 'how,' I can't rightly tell. Must be something I ate."

She sounded so miserable that Marcus immediately set himself to comfort her.

"Now, now, dear girl," he said briskly. "You must look upon the bright side. The, er, boy—it is a boy? Yes—is a magnificent specimen of mousehood, beyond any shadow of doubt. A great credit to you, Maddie my love, very great." He paused. "Very great indeed," he went on absently.

"Yes, but what about t'others, poor little mites?"

"Ah," said Marcus. "The others. Yes. Indeed. Well, my dear, it would appear to me that their chances of survival are, to say the least of it, thin, very thin." He paused. "Very thin indeed," he mused.

"Talk plain," said Madeleine perplexedly. "D'you mean you think the other five are going to . . . ?"

"Snuff it," said Marcus Aurelius shortly. And by next morning they had.

At sunrise Marcus left the cottage through a hole that emerged behind a stone flower trough by the back door, and ran down the garden path toward the pigsty. Unable to stand the sight of the five weakening babies and, especially, the one that seemed to grow larger and stronger by the minute, he had spent the night alone in his newspaper bed, much of it in deep thought.

Always his mind came back to Madeleine's words. "Must be something I ate," she had said.

The pigsty was really a double one, but the cottagers, since they only ever fattened one pig at a time, used the other half of the covered-in section as a food store. In spring and summertime the mice found this an admirable arrangement, but in the autumn the pig would disappear, they never knew where, and there would be no food in the store.

Now, as Marcus ran up the drainhole into the sty, there was nothing in the outer run but a lingering smell of disinfectant. Inside was the empty staging, and, next door, the food store, swept clean of the last particles of barley meal.

But on top of one of the meal bins, Marcus noticed, was a large cardboard packet, and he ran up the wall and scuttled across to look at it.

At first he could not decipher the printed writing on it, but then he realized it had been left upside down. He hung head downward from the top of it, balancing himself with his long tail, and could now clearly read it:

Pennyfeather's Patent Porker Pills
Add one pill per day to a normal fattening ration
You will be amazed at the weight gain

There followed a long selection of extracts from letters from satisfied users and a list of the various ingredients of the pills, and then finally a single sentence, printed in red capitals:

WARNING: DO NOT EXCEED THE STATED DOSE

"Oh no," said Marcus Aurelius to himself, "she could not have done so foolish a thing. Surely not? No, no, the packet is unopened. They cannot long have bought it. It must be for next year's pig."

He slid down the packet and ran all round it. And there, in the back bottom corner, was a small hole, a hole which something had nibbled, a hole which, as he nudged at it with his nose, expelled one round shiny white pill, the size of an aspirin.

Marcus ran out of the pigsty and back up the path to the cottage. So preoccupied was he with his whirling thoughts that he almost bumped into the cat as it came out of the flap in the back door.

Once in the family home he confronted his wife as she lay and nursed the giant child, alone now in the nest.

"Maddie my dear," said Marcus Aurelius. "Recently, that is to say in our summer residence, did you eat anything at all out of the ordinary?"

"I don't think so, Markie," replied Madeleine. "Though of course we all do tend to fancy some funny things at these times. No, just barley meal, bit of flaked maize, the pick of the pigswill. Oh, wait a minute though. There was a cardboard packet on top of the bin, had some big round sweets in it. I opened it up myself just about the time these babies—this baby, I do mean, oh, dear!—was started. I fancied them, Markie, they was nice! I ate one every day."

"Oh, Maddie, Maddie!" said Marcus Aurelius, more in sorrow than in anger. "Did you not read what was written on that packet?"

"Don't be silly, Markie dear," said Madeleine comfortably. "You knows I can't read."

CHAPTER 2

Nasty Cat!

If only Madeleine had let well enough alone. If, that is, you could say that things were well, when the monster baby mouse, now three weeks old, was already almost as big as his mother and constantly, incessantly, demanding food.

At first Madeleine tried to manage alone, not wishing to disturb Marcus Aurelius from his regular routine of reading and contemplation, but the strain of constant foraging to supplement her dwindling milk supply was too much for her; and soon both parents were continually on the run, searching everywhere for anything remotely edible to offer to the ravenous baby, like two little birds feeding a cuckoo child.

But if only Madeleine could have left it at that. Perhaps they would have managed somehow. Perhaps the creature would not have become much larger, for its rate of growth did seem to be slowing down.

As it was, there came a morning when she said to her husband, tiredly (for they had been up all night scavenging), "It's no good, Markie, we'll have to try those sweets."

"Sweets, my dear?" panted Marcus Aurelius, breathless from the effort of dragging into the nest a

crust of bread, fallen from the cottagers' table. "What sweets?"

"The ones in that packet," said Madeleine. "The ones I was telling you about. Down at our summer house. You know. I took them. When I was expecting. I found them ever so filling, so maybe they'd fill him up."

Marcus peered consideringly at their son, who had already devoured most of the bread and was chomping his way through what was left with ceaselessly moving jaws.

"Ah, the Porker Pills, my dear. Ahum. Would you really consider such a course of action to be wise?"

"Dunno about wise," said Madeleine. "But we'd be fools not to try it. I'm fair working my claws to the bone for him. Listen to him now." The huge baby, his crust finished, was making loud use of his first and favorite word.

9

"More!" he yelled. "More! More!"

"Well, Maddie," said Marcus Aurelius, "you may be right. But you must also ask yourself whether, in view of the season of the year and the sheer physical difficulties of transporting the material, such a course is practicable?"

"Come again?"

"Can we do it? Can we, in short, bunt, butt, shunt, shove or otherwise propel such an awkward object as a Porker Pill all the way up the path in the wind and rain? I make no mention of the cat."

"Mebbe not," said Madeleine, "but we don't have to. We'll go back down there, to the pigsty. And then he can make a proper pig of himself."

"It will be very cold," said Marcus doubtfully, for his newspaper nest in the sitting-room wall was no more than three feet from the fireplace and beautifully warm in winter.

"It won't be for long," said Madeleine. "He'll soon be able to look after himself and then we can come back indoors. And there's another thing. We'll have to get him out of here soon anyways or he won't never get out. He'll be too big."

Some days later, when they made the move, the truth of Madeleine's words was plain to see, for it took the combined efforts of both parents to force the massive body of their child through the hole behind the stone flower trough. They had chosen their moment carefully. The cottagers were at work at the other end of the garden, and the cat, Marcus had carefully noted, was asleep in front of the sitting-room fire. Madeleine made haste down the path, calling to her son to follow, for he was inclined to linger and investigate the strange sights and smells of the outside world. Behind him Marcus Aurelius fussed and fretted, anxious to be under cover. In his agitation he actually resorted to the use of slang.

"Skedaddle, lad!" he cried to the lumbering infant. "Stir your stumps! Look lively! Put your foot down! Get your skates on! Step on the gas!"

"He means 'hurry!' " cried Madeleine over her shoulder.

As they neared safety a strange thing happened. A blackbird, disturbed from the nearby hedge, flew suddenly low over the three mice with a loud cry of alarm. Madeleine shot into the drainhole of the sty while Marcus instinctively froze in his tracks. But the great baby, far from showing fear, made an angry leap at the bird as it passed and chattered shrilly with rage, his little jaws clacking together upon the empty air.

Once inside the food store the parents' first action was to nose out from the packet one of Pennyfeather's Patent Porker Pills. Having rolled it onto the floor, they maneuvered it under the wooden staging, where their waiting child immediately fell upon it with little grunts of greed. They watched him, awestruck.

"Do you know, Maddie," said Marcus Aurelius in a low voice, "that not only was he not frightened by that blackbird, but he actually tried to assail it?"

"Assail it?"

"Attack it. Have a go at it."

"Never!"

"He did, I give you my word."

Madeleine shook her head in bewilderment as they watched this strange son of theirs gorging upon the Porker Pill.

"He hasn't got a name, Markie," she said in a distracted voice. "I was thinking just now, when I called him to hurry. We must give him a name, it don't make no sense to go on calling him Baby like I've been doing."

"Very true, my dear," said Marcus. "Undoubtedly he needs a name befitting his great size."

"Well, that ought to be easy enough," said Madeleine. "I remember you telling me your family nest was lined with pages from dictionaries and lexicons and suchlike when you was up at Oxford. What's the Latin for 'great'?"

"Magnus."

"Magnus," said Madeleine consideringly. "I like the sound of that. Yes. We'll call him Magnus." And as if to celebrate the occasion, the newly named Magnus set up his customary cry of "More! More!" and off went his parents to fetch another pill.

By midday he had eaten three. He lay, sated and asleep at last, in the old summer nest of hay and straw and dried moss, and it seemed to Madeleine and Marcus Aurelius that he had grown appreciably in size since the morning. A fourth Porker Pill was clasped in his powerful forearms, ready for the moment of waking.

"They don't seem to have done him no harm," said Madeleine.

"Certainly that voracious appetite would seem, if only temporarily, to have been gratified," said Marcus.

"You mean he's had enough."

"Just so. Indeed it occurs to me that, were we to supply the boy—"

"Magnus."

"—were we to supply Magnus with an adequate ration—a dozen of these things should last him for some long time—we might leave him here and return to the cottage. I find this place distinctly chilly."

"Chilly?" said Madeleine in a voice that was positively icy. "Marcus Aurelius, you find it chilly, do you?"

Marcus flinched inwardly at her use of his full and proper name, a sure sign of trouble, but he persisted bravely. "Indeed I do, my dear. I am no longer a young mouse, you know."

"But Magnus," said Madeleine distinctly, "is a young mouse. A very young mouse. Don't you think he might find it chilly? All by himself?"

"I doubt it, my dear," said Marcus earnestly. "The young do not feel the cold as we older ones do. And the boy, er, Magnus, that is, has a thick coat of hair now, very thick." He paused. "Very thick indeed."

"Marcus Aurelius!"

"Yes, dear?"

"Beat it!"

"I beg your pardon, my dear?"

"Push off!" said Madeleine angrily.

"But . . . what about you?"

"Me? I shall stay with little Magnus of course," said Madeleine, and she ranged herself protectively alongside the sleeping infant, now nearly twice her size.

Marcus Aurelius was sorely tempted to leave. The afternoon air was indeed cold, and the picture of himself curled up in his fireside nest with an interesting extract from *The Somerset Guardian* was clear in his mind. But what he would have decided was not to be known, for at that moment there was a heavy thump on the wooden staging above their heads, and the air of the pigsty was filled with the strong reek of cat.

The sleeping baby awoke. His first action was to take a bite from the pill which he held, but, this done, he raised a questing nose.

"Nasty!" said Magnus loudly.

"Shhh, dear," whispered Madeleine, "it's only an old cat. Just you keep still and quiet, there's a good boy."

"Nasty cat!" said Magnus with a shout, and the tip of the cat's tail, which hung down between a crack in the boards as it sat directly above them, twitched sharply at the sound of the squeak.

"Your mother is right, Magnus," said Marcus Aurelius in a low voice. "Our best course of action is to preserve silence and to remain unmoving. We are quite safe in our present location. Eventually, if I do not miss my guess, and I may tell you that I have a vast amount of experience in these matters, very vast—" he paused, "—very vast indeed—eventually, as I was saying, the creature will fall victim to boredom—"

"So shall us all," said Madeleine under her breath.

"—and go away."

"Bite you!!" yelled Magnus at the top of his voice.

"No, it won't bite you, my love," said Madeleine soothingly. "It can't get in under here, you see, it's too—" But before she could finish Magnus threw aside his pill and rose stiff-legged from the nest, his eyes snapping, his coat hair standing on end.

"Bite you!!" he cried again, and leaping forward, he fastened his needle teeth in the dangling tail tip.

There was a split second of absolute silence and then an explosion of sound and movement above. Madeleine and Marcus Aurelius stared at one another in horror. Of Magnus there was no sign.

CHAPTER 3

The Ghost

W hen the startled cat shot up in the air with a yowl and out of the sty and over the wall, Magnus hung on like grim death. And grim death—for him—it most certainly would have been but for one of those quirks of Fate that rule our lives.

The cat's leap caught the eye of the dog from the cottage next door, a small fierce terrier which spent many of its waking hours patrolling the rusty chain-link fence that separated the two properties. Whenever it saw its ancient enemy it bounced furiously against the fence, hoping against hope that one day the wire would disintegrate and let it through. And on this occasion it did.

Halfway down the garden path the cat had stopped to investigate the cause of the pain in its tail tip. The paw that scooped Magnus neatly from his hold was midway to its mouth when the terrier appeared at top speed.

Dropped abruptly by the cat and promptly trampled upon by the charging dog, the unfortunate baby was left breathless and dizzy. His spirit, however, had not deserted him, for he ground his little teeth in anger and still muttered "Bite you! Bite you!" in a small strangled voice. He picked himself up and made unsteadily for the nearest shelter, which happened to be the greenhouse. Its sliding door was open a few inches and through it Magnus crawled.

A moment later the dog came rushing back, tail between legs and hotly pursued by the cottagers in defense of their cat. There followed a good deal of noise—the cat owners shouting at the dog owners, the dog owners shouting back, and the dog barking loudly from the safety of his own garden—and then Magnus heard the sound of footsteps coming back down the path, and of grumbly voices. "Them and their dratted dog!" and "I'll shoot him. See if I don't!" and then "Pull the greenhouse door to, will you?"

There was a scraping noise and a thud, and Magnus was a prisoner.

For some time he did not realize that he could not get out. As usual, his first thought, once he had caught his breath, was of food, and food to him at present meant anything he could put in his mouth. "Nasty! Nasty! Nasty!" cried Magnus as he spat out in turn mouthfuls of peat, of potting compost and of fertilizer granules. But then he came upon a great pile of dahlia bulbs laid out to dry, and finding the flavor pleasant, settled down to the biggest one.

Soon it was dark outside, and Madeleine and Marcus Aurelius prepared to make their sorrowing way back indoors.

"Oh, Markie, Markie," said Madeleine for the

umpteenth time. "D'you think he could still be alive, somehow?"

"Try to compose yourself, Maddie dear," said Marcus patiently. "The chances of his survival are, as I have said, extremely remote. Any mouse, it is painfully clear to me, that is attached to the tail of a cat pursued by a dog, must be, to say the least, and with no attempt to mince words, in dire trouble, very dire." He paused. "Very dire indeed."

"And him so little," cried Madeleine.

"Hardly so little," said Marcus. "He was already far larger than either of us."

But Madeleine could by no means be comforted by the thought of her son's stature at the moment of death, and it was some time before she could be persuaded to come out of the pigsty into the night.

"Suppose we finds him!" she said in sudden terror. "Suppose we finds him left by the path, poor little soul?"

"Highly unlikely," said Marcus Aurelius judiciously. "He will undoubtedly have already been—" he was about to say "eaten" but hurriedly changed it to "laid to rest."

"Oh, Markie, I'm feared to go up that path!"

"Nonsense, my dear, I will go first. There is no reason to be afraid."

But Madeleine was, and as she tiptoed up the garden path behind the scuttling Marcus Aurelius her eyes were out on stalks, searching the black night for some unknown horror.

Inside the greenhouse Magnus was in all sorts of trouble. He had gorged upon the dahlia bulb until he became very thirsty; on the floor was an old metal watering can, full, and in drinking from this he had lost his balance and fallen in; it was only his unusual strength that allowed him somehow to scramble out again, soaked to the skin, whereupon he promptly blundered into a brown paper bag of garden lime and was plastered in it from head to toe, white as snow. Finally, he had at last discovered that he was shut in, and was raging around in a perfect fury.

At the very moment that Madeleine was passing the greenhouse, every nerve stretched tight, Magnus was standing in the darkness not a yard from her. He stood upon his hind legs, his forefeet pressed against

the inside of the closed glass door, his mouth wide open in a furious yell of frustration and anger. And at that instant the moon swam out from behind the clouds and shone full upon him.

Madeleine's squeal of terror was so loud as to be heard by Marcus Aurelius who was already safely in the family home behind the larder, and not many seconds later she came tumbling in after him.

"Oh, Markie, Markie!" cried Madeleine breathlessly. "I seen him!"

"Seen . . . that is to say, saw whom?"

"Our Magnus! Oh, it was horrible, what I seen!"

"You saw his . . . body?"

"No! No!"

"What then?"

"His ghost! Oh, crumbs, Markie, you wouldn't believe how horrible it was! He was stood up on two legs like a human, and his little hands was spread out, asking for help, and he was calling to me—I could see though I couldn't hear nothing—and his hair was all spiky like a hedgehog's. But what was worst of all, he was white, white as a sheet from tip to tail. Oh, Markie, 'twas his ghost all right, oh, oh, oh, oh, oh, oh!!!" And Madeleine went off into such a fit of screaming hysterics that the cottagers came into the kitchen and opened the larder door.

"Just listen to them," said the man to his wife. "Dratted mice! You'd think they owned the place, they're so noisy. It's time to get the traps out."

CHAPTER 4

Too Too Solid Flesh

Inside his trap Magnus was in quite a state. During the night he had fallen once more into the watering can, washing off most of the lime but becoming as a result extremely muddy as he rampaged around the earthen floor looking for a way of escape. His tousled coat clogged with soil, he now looked more like a half-grown sewer rat than a baby mouse. He was also very angry.

In the middle of the morning the woman came down the garden path to open the sliding door a little, for the November weather was unusually mild, and the humidity in the greenhouse, she knew, would do her plants no good. No sooner had she put a carpet-slippered foot inside than, to her horror, it was pounced upon by a fierce animal, the like of which she had never seen before, which gave a high-pitched growl and sank its teeth into her ankle.

"Nasty! Nasty!" cried Magnus indistinctly through clenched jaws, "Bite you!" before a frantic kick sent him flying, and his chatters of rage mingled with the frightened cries of his victim as she hastily limped back up the path to fetch her husband. But when they returned a few moments later, each armed with a stout

23

stick, there was no sign of her attacker. Only the pile of half-eaten dahlia bulbs told its own tale.

"Must have been a rat," said the man.

"Not like any rat I ever saw."

"Fetch the cat. He might follow it."

But like all its kind the cat had no desire to do what humans wished it to, and only stalked away again, tail twitching.

Magnus meantime had found his way back to the pigsty. His anger had been replaced by his other chief emotion, greed. He had also acquired a new word to supplement his meager vocabulary.

"Nice," murmured Magnus, as he laid into a Porker Pill with a noise like splintering bones. "Nice. Nice."

Inside the cottage Madeleine and Marcus Aurelius were breakfasting, with distinct lack of appetite.

"To think," said Madeleine in a broken voice, "yesterday he was here with us. And now . . ."

"There, there, Maddie my dear," said Marcus. "There will be others."

"But not like him."

"True," said Marcus. "Very true." He paused reflectively. "Very true indeed," he said.

"Oh, my poor baby . . ."

"Magnus," put in Marcus absently.

"My poor Magnus. There'll never be another like him, never!"

"Highly improbable."

"Oh, Markie!" cried Madeleine. "A mouse's life is

not a happy one!" Marcus Aurelius looked about to dispute this sweeping statement, but before he could begin, Madeleine went on, "Maybe it's a good thing, him going from this vale of tears so young. Who knows what he might have been spared. If 'twasn't the cat, it mighta bin poison. Or traps. And that reminds me, Markie, the trapping season's started, they put 'em out last night, did you notice?"

"To be honest, my dear, no. I came across a most interesting cutting from the *Bristol Evening Post*, on the manufacture of Cheddar cheese, and—"

"Marcus Aurelius!" said Madeleine. "You mean you sat there calmly reading? After what happened last night? How could you?"

"The traps, Maddie dear," said Marcus hastily. "Where are they?"

"Usual places," said Madeleine. "Under the sink. Larder floor. Linen closet. And usual bait—bacon rind. Got no imagination, they haven't."

"Fortunately, my dear," said Marcus, "only unusually foolish mice become involved with such contraptions."

"Or unusually shortsighted ones," said Madeleine, and flounced out of the nest.

What with grief for her lost son and irritation with her insensitive husband, she was halfway down the garden path, opposite the greenhouse, before she came to her senses. A shiver of fear ran through her as she forced herself to peer hastily through the glass but no mouthing ghost stood imploringly within. Then the cat flap in the back door squeaked on its hinges and Madeleine fled for the pigsty and the happiest moment of her little life so far. For there, beneath the staging, stood a very substantial, very dirty, very beloved figure.

"Mummy! Nice Mummy!" cried Magnus loudly. "More! More!"

Madeleine spent the rest of the day there, dividing her time between fetching down stocks of Porker Pills, cleaning up her muddied child, and simply lying and feasting her eyes upon him in a daze of happiness. She was quite unable to understand how he had escaped what had seemed certain death, since Magnus's replies to all her questioning consisted only of "Nasty!" "Nice," or "Bite you!" with an occasional "More!" thrown in, but she did not care. All that mattered was that he was there, twice as large as life.

Four weeks passed, during which time Magnus doubled not only his age but his size. What a limitless diet of Pennyfeather's Patent Porker Pills would have done to a pig heaven only knows, but there was no doubt what it was doing to a mouse. Magnus was by now almost the size of a rat and still going strong. Indeed one day an old yellow-toothed bare-tailed buck rat had come upon Magnus unexpectedly under the pigsty flooring and had fled from the strange young giant with a squeal of terror.

As for Madeleine, she needed to look lively whenever she heard the warning cry of "Nice Mummy!"

For Magnus was an affectionate and demonstrative child, and nimble footwork was needed if she were not to be crushed beneath the weight of his nuzzling love.

Fortunately it was a mild winter, as she had firmly decided to stay down at the summer home until he should be fully grown. "Whatever that may mean," she said to herself with a worried shake of the head. The night cold did not trouble her, since sleeping beside Magnus kept her warm as toast. She slept very lightly however, fearing to be squashed flat.

Only once had Marcus Aurelius come back down to the pigsty, on the evening of that first day after the episode with the cat. Madeleine had come rushing into his fireside nest with the news that the supposed ghost was in fact solid flesh. "Too too solid!" Marcus had cried plaintively, recoiling hastily before his son's caresses.

Something told Madeleine that her husband's principal emotion, should he now set eyes upon the two-month-old Magnus, would not be, as hers was, pride, but horror. She left him to his reading.

Meanwhile she busied herself with Magnus's education. The day's supply of Porker Pills prepared, the little mother would sit before her mighty child and teach him the rules that govern the lives of mice, the rules of survival. She had been taught them in the nest by her mother and so back through hundreds of generations, so that they were couched in old-fashioned language.

Some were in the form of proverbs. "Look thou before thou leapest," "A squeak in time saveth nine," or "Through whatsoever hole thy whiskers pass, there will thy body also." Magnus made little response to such maxims, merely staring stolidly at Madeleine, his jaws champing ceaselessly. He much preferred a series of commandments, which his mother would repeat to him each morning, all beginning with the words "Beware thou the . . ."

The list was a long one: "Beware thou the trap . . . the poison bait . . . the man . . . the dog . . . the owl . . . the weasel," and so on. During this recitation Magnus would become increasingly excited, ears pricked, eyes snapping, until at the last commandment, "Beware thou the cat," he would give a great shout of "Nasty!"

Madeleine tried hard to teach him to repeat these lessons after her, but, though his vocabulary was certainly increasing, he could still only put two words together at any one time. The commonest two were "Pill, Mummy!" and the day came when Madeleine, rooting at the hole in the bottom of the packet, realized that there were very few of Mr. Pennyfeather's products left.

That night she made the dangerous trip back to the cottage to consult her learned husband on the matter.

"What shall us do, Markie?" she cried agitatedly. "I shall never manage to find enough food for our Magnus once they pills is gone. You'll have to come down and help."

Marcus Aurelius controlled his immediate reaction, which was to refuse point-blank to do any such thing. He had no desire to leave the safety and comfort of his den and face danger and hardship in order to fill the huge belly of this demanding cuckoo child. Nearly three months old, he thought angrily, and still relying on his mother for everything. Why, at that age I was completely self-sufficient, knew my way about the entire college from buttery to refectory. On the other hand, he did not wish his wife to be exposed to further risk, for he knew she would continue to try to find food whether he helped or no. He combed his whiskers thoughtfully.

"Well, Maddie my dear," he said at last, "it appears to me that there is only one answer."

"What's that then?"

"Emigration."

"Emi-what?"

"Emigration, my dear. The boy, er, Magnus, must leave home, seek his fortune, go out into the wide world—possibly to the farm across the road, there should be plenty to eat there."

"Marcus . . . Aurelius!"

"Yes, dear?"

"Are you serious?"

"Serious, dear?"

"Are you seriously telling me that we should kick out our only child—"

"Hardly our only child, dear," interrupted Marcus.

"—to be eaten by farm cats, chewed up by farm dogs, hit on the head by farm workers, squashed flat by farm tractors?"

"It is to be hoped that none of these fates will befall him."

"Marcus . . . Aurelius!"

"Yes, dear?"

"Are you saying he's got to go?"

"Yes, dear."

"Over my dead body!"

"That's what it will be over, Maddie," said Marcus earnestly, "if he stays. And mine, too, if you insist. The boy is obviously too big to get back into the house, the pills are almost finished, just think of the constant dangers to which you . . . to which we shall be exposed while attempting to satisfy his appetite. The only possible way in which he might stay with us, within the confines of the garden, that is, would depend upon the discovery of an alternative source of supply of suitable food near at hand."

Madeleine let out a sudden squeak. "The rabbit!" she cried excitedly.

"I beg your pardon?"

"The rabbit! That lives in that big hutch. In the opposite corner from the pigsty. Beyond the plum trees."

"Oh, come, Maddie my dear," said Marcus in a patient tone of voice. "Granted that mice are omnivorous, I take leave to doubt that Magnus could kill and eat a full-grown rabbit."

"No, not eat the rabbit, Markie," cried Madeleine impatiently. "Eat the rabbit's food! They buys it for him, lovely stuff it is, oats and bran and flaked maize and little special pellets. Of course, of course, that's the answer."

Marcus Aurelius heaved an inward sigh of relief. The problem seemed to be solved, and he was anxious to return to his reading. Madeleine had interrupted him in the middle of an absorbing scrap torn from the *Farmer & Stockbreeder*.

"Come on then, Markie!"

"Come on?"

"Down to the rabbit hutch. We must see about getting Magnus's breakfast, there's no time to waste."

"But—"

"Marcus Aurelius!"

So out into the night they went.

As dawn broke they were crouched side by side underneath an old table on which stood the rabbit hutch. They had passed the rest of the night in the pigsty, and Marcus Aurelius was nursing his bruises, for his son had stepped on him. "Nice Daddy!" Magnus had roared at the sight of him and, rushing affectionately forward, had crushed his shortsighted little sire beneath his huge feet.

In addition both were shivering, with cold, and with fear, for this was a comparatively unknown part of the garden, and the gray light showed strange shapes all about.

At that moment the dawn wind brought clearly to their ears a plaintive cry from the pigsty, for the last of Pennyfeather's Patent Porker Pills was eaten.

"More, Mummy!" yelled Magnus. "More! More!"

"Come on then, Markie," said Madeleine grimly, and she ran up the table leg to the rabbit hutch.

CHAPTER 5

Uncle Roland

The rabbit was a large one. It was white in color and it had very long floppy ears, which lay upon the hutch floor at right angles to its head. The effect of those flattened ears combined with a stare from a pair of eyes of the brightest red to give the creature a very strange look.

Madeleine's little heart thumped madly as she confronted it. She looked around for support and finding none, peeped over the edge of the table. Marcus was still on the ground, obviously extremely nervous by the way he hopped from foot to foot. Indeed it was now broad light and not a good time for mice to be out in a danger-filled garden.

But though the cries of "More!" had ceased to come from the pigsty, their echoes were clear in Madeleine's ears, and she did not think about her personal safety.

"Marcus Aurelius!" she cried sharply. "Come up here this instant!" And she turned to the rabbit.

As she met the unblinking stare of those red eyes, various approaches flashed through her mind. She could threaten it. But with what? She could cajole it, plead with it, go down on her haunches and beg. But she was too proud. She could raid the hutch, slip through the wire netting, grab some grub and run, dodging whatever offensive action the great beast might take. But this would have to be repeated a hundred times to satisfy Magnus's appetite.

It was the look in the red eyes that finally made her decide upon a straightforward statement of fact. It was a friendly look, she felt sure.

"Look, mister or missus," she said simply and firmly, "we'm in trouble." At this point Marcus Aurelius arrived beside her. He had bumped his head, not seeing the overhang of the table edge as he had run up the

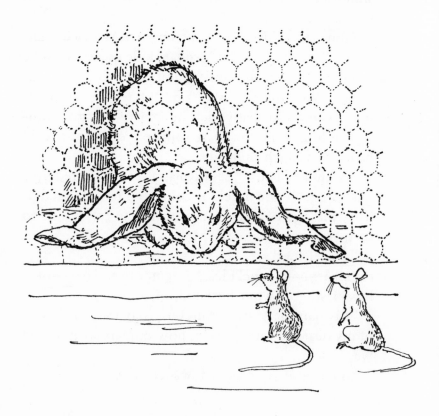

leg, and could only stare dazedly into the hutch, out of words for once.

The rabbit hopped to the front of its hutch. At close range both mice could see that it had a kindly face.

"I'm sorry about that," it said in a deep voice. "And it's mister actually. Roland's the name. Tell me now, what's biting you?"

Marcus Aurelius gave an uneasy giggle. "Nothing, sir," he said. "At this moment, that is to say. Though if one considers the number of possible enemies all anxious to sink their teeth, claws, beaks or talons into us—"

"Bide quiet, Markie!" interrupted Madeleine angrily. "For the love of Cheddar, bide quiet, or I'll be sinking my teeth in you!" She turned to the rabbit. "Look, Mr. Roland," she said. "I'll tell you straight, no messing. Our baby, he's hungry, we've got nothing for him. Can you spare some of your grub? We'd be ever so much obliged."

"A hungry baby!" said Roland softly, his red eyes glistening. "Poor mite! Of course I'd be delighted to help, they give me far more than I can eat. Come to that, please do come in, Mrs. . . . ?"

"Madeleine."

"Charming name! Please do come in and have some breakfast. And your husband, of course, Mr. . . . ?"

"My name is Marcus Aurelius. May I say, on behalf of my dear wife and myself, how immensely gratified we—"

"Shut your trap!" cried Madeleine in a fury.

36

Not surprisingly, this particular phrase is seldom used in mouse conversation, and it reduced the voluble Marcus to immediate tight-lipped silence.

Roland's pink nose twitched uncontrollably for a moment, and then he said soothingly, "Why not run and fetch the little chap first of all, and then we'll all eat together, eh?"

Madeleine shot a glance at her husband and saw

that he was sulking. For an instant she considered ordering him to fetch Magnus but then common sense prevailed. He would probably debate the matter at great length, he would take ten times as long over the journey as she, he would run blindly into danger. Anyway she already felt bad about having snapped at him in front of a stranger.

"Pop in through the wire then, Markie," she said. "I shan't be a minute." She slid down the table leg and bounded away toward the pigsty, her long tail spiraling to keep her balance in the rough grass beneath the plum trees.

"How fortunate you are to have such a spirited wife," said Roland. "I myself have never experienced marriage."

"It has its ups and downs," said Marcus Aurelius.

"No doubt. But to have children—an infinite blessing, one would imagine."

"They can be a great trial," said Marcus. "Very great." He paused. "Very great indeed," he said.

"You surprise me. I myself came from a very large litter. I have always supposed that somewhere or other I have by now a host of nephews and nieces. I have often fancied being called Uncle Roland."

"I dare say Magnus would oblige."

"Magnus?"

"My son. It should not be beyond him. He can just about string two words together," said Marcus sourly.

"Dear little fellow! I cannot wait to see him," said Roland. "But do please come in and make a start."

Marcus was about to explain that "little" was a word which could not be applied to his son when he realized that there was no possible way for Magnus to squeeze through the wire mesh that he himself had slipped so easily between.

But at that moment there was a scrabbling of claws and Madeleine appeared, her black eyes almost bolting out of her head. "Oh, Markie, Markie," she cried brokenly, "he ain't there!"

"He *isn't* there," said Marcus in correction.

"That's what I'm telling you. Don't just repeat it. The pigsty's empty. Where can he be?"

Marcus Aurelius particularly liked being asked this kind of question, which demanded a variety of precise, carefully thought out answers. He raised his head consideringly from the rabbit's feeding pot.

"Let us see," he said. "A. He could have gone to the cottage, looking for us. Here, however, his only possible means of entry would appear to be the cat flap. This might present a problem. Or B. He could have taken that course of action of which I spoke to you last night, and emigrated. To the farm perhaps, or elsewhere. Or C. He could be wandering about the garden, in quest of food. I make no mention of D."

"What d'you mean? What's D?"

"You must be brave, Maddie; I would spare your feelings if I were able. But the fourth likelihood is that he could have been carried off."

"Carried off?"

39

"By some carnivorous beast—D stands for Death," said Marcus Aurelius in his clipped voice, and he fell once more to eating.

Madeleine looked so woebegone that the soft-hearted Roland's eyes began once more to glisten.

"Come inside, Madeleine," he said in his deep growl. "Come and have some food, you'll feel better then. I'm sure nothing has happened to your Magnus. He's probably quite safe, down a hole."

"It would have to be a rabbit hole," said Marcus with his mouth full.

"I don't understand."

"He's rather . . . big," said Madeleine.

"A baby, I thought you said?"

"Well, he ain't very old—only three months—but he growed, you see, he growed ever so fast."

"You mean," said Roland, "he's bigger than the average mouse?"

"Yes," said Madeleine, "much bigger. In fact . . ."

"Yes?"

Madeleine was silent for a moment. Part of her did not want to finish what she had been going to say, and part of her cried out, Go on! Spit it out! Say it out loud, in front of this stranger, get it over with, say the word, you'll be the better for it.

She took a deep breath.

"In fact," said Madeleine, "Magnus is a giant."

Afterward Madeleine never quite knew what reaction she had expected to this statement. Simple disbelief, perhaps? Or pity? Or disgust? What she had not been prepared for was the tremendous stamp of excitement which the rabbit gave with his hind feet upon the floorboards of the hutch, causing Marcus Aurelius to shoot up into the air like a trampolinist.

"A giant!" roared Roland. "How perfectly splendid!"

"Splendid?"

"Why, yes, indeed, giantism, in rabbits at any rate, is a most honorable condition. Why, one of our oldest and best respected breeds is the Flemish Giant. I myself am the product of a marriage between two of the giant breeds, for my father was a Lop and my mother a New Zealand White. Oh, my dear Madeleine, how proud you must be!"

Even in the midst of her worries Madeleine felt a glow at these words, a glow, she quickly realized, that was indeed of pride. Giants were respectable then!

"Oh, how kind of you, Mr. Roland, I'm sure!" she said. "Wait till you meet him! And he's so affectionate, too! You'll see!" She paused, and her whiskers twitched with anxiety. "I hopes," she said softly.

All this time Madeleine had been looking into the hutch and Marcus into the feeding pot. Only Roland was looking out toward the garden, and now he suddenly said, "Tell me. Would your Magnus be . . . as big as a rat?"

"Bigger."

"Big as a guinea pig?"

"Never seen one of they."

"Well, I don't want to raise your hopes wrongly,

but there is a guinea-pig-sized animal, mouse-colored, with a tail, somewhere in the Brussels sprouts. I caught a glimpse of it just a moment ago."

Madeleine whipped round and Marcus left the feeding pot, and into the forest of sprout plants that stood directly between the hutch and the back door of the cottage peered three pairs of eyes, one black and snapping, one red and shining, one myopic and watery. And sure enough, as they watched, out from the vegetable patch came Magnus, and out from Magnus came a mighty voice. "Mummy!" it bellowed. "More! More! More!"

There was a moment's breathless silence and then one other sound, coming clearly to their ears on the still cold air. It was the squeak of the cat flap!

CHAPTER 6

Magnus Earns His Name

When Magnus had finished the last of the Porker Pills which his mother had put ready for him the previous day, his first action was of course to yell for more. Receiving no response (for his parents were even then confronting the rabbit), he squeezed his bulk out from under the staging in the pigsty and went next door. There on top of the meal bin stood the magic packet, and Magnus's greed drove him to make the climb up to it for the first time in his spoiled young life. It was empty.

In fury and frustration Magnus ripped the cardboard packet to bits with his razor-sharp teeth. He leaped down and dashed angrily into the garden, and in the wind of his passing a scrap of cardboard blew off the bin and fluttered gently down to the ground: *You will be amazed at the weight gain*, it read.

At first Magnus ran aimlessly about the cottage garden, his uplifted nose searching the air for food smells. He found a very small piece of fat that had fallen from the bird table, and one, the last, of the previous season's apple fallings, half rotten, but apart from these there were only vegetables—spring cabbages, winter-sown broad beans, and Brussels sprouts.

43

Among these last he stopped and shouted his usual request.

Instinctively, when the cat flap squeaked, Madeleine shot in through the wire of the hutch door, but it was Magnus's safety that she was immediately concerned for.

"Quickly, my baby!" she cried at the top of her voice. "Over here! Run over here! We be both in the rabbit hutch!"

"We *are* both in the rabbit hutch," said Marcus Aurelius.

"I knows that, stupid!" said Madeleine exasperatedly. "We wants to get our Magnus in here, too."

"How?" said Marcus.

"Your husband has a point," said Roland. "Now that one has actually seen your boy, one begins to realize the problems involved. Is there nowhere else he could seek safety?"

Before Madeleine could answer, the cat came round the corner of the cottage. Immediately it caught sight of Magnus and it stood up very tall, its ears pricked. Then it bounded into the Brussels sprout forest.

In the hutch all was confusion and noise as Roland gave a series of warning thumps with his hind feet and scrabbled madly but fruitlessly at the wire with his forepaws, while the little mice bombarded their son with frantic advice.

"Run for the pigsty!"

"Run for the tool shed!"

"Run for the greenhouse!"

"Run for the coal-hole!"

"Run, Magnus! For the love of Cheddar, run!!"

And through all the hubbub Magnus stood staring blankly at them all, confused by the noise and unaware of the danger.

Then Roland's deep voice rang out above. "Behind you, lad!" he thundered. "Look behind you!"

And as Magnus whirled, the cat came creeping on its elbows out of the sprout forest, its ears flat to its head, the tip of that once-bitten tail twitching.

As the ancient Romans at the Coliseum looked down upon some wretched Christian awaiting the lion, so the three spectators in the rabbit hutch stared down upon the sacrificial scene. For though, unlike the Romans, they did not wish the cat to slay its helpless victim, they knew, like them, that inevitably it would.

"Oh, my poor baby," whispered Madeleine.

"Forever and forever, farewell, Magnus!" murmured Marcus Aurelius.

"Brave lad!" growled Roland softly. "He did not cut and run."

And silence fell.

Slowly, nightmarishly slowly, the cat crept forward, until it was no more than a dozen feet from Magnus. It stopped and crouched, and the watchers waited helplessly for the final lightning rush and pounce, the remorseless end to every ordinary cat-and-mouse affair.

But though the cat was ordinary, the mouse was

not. Magnus did not run, did not retreat an inch. Rather did he move a step toward the enemy, and as he did so his coat rose on end, with fright one might have thought, making him appear even bigger. But it was not fright, it was anger.

Tulip-eared, harsh-coated, his long tail stiffly out behind him like a pointing dog, he moved a fraction nearer still. And the silence was broken.

"Nasty cat," said Magnus distinctly, in a voice made all the more compelling by its unnatural quietness. "Nasty cat. Bite you."

At these words a shudder of excitement passed through the three spectators, for two of them (Marcus was too shortsighted) saw the effect they had had upon

the cat. It was, they saw, discomfited and suddenly it could not meet the approaching Magnus's gaze. Very slowly, very slightly, it turned its head, so that its golden eyes were focused not upon Magnus, not upon the watchers in the hutch, but, by chance, upon the pigsty.

Now there is no knowing whether the cat could have remembered that painful incident of two months past, or whether, if it had, it would have connected the baby mouse scraped so casually off its tail tip with the hulking threatening monster that was now not merely confronting but actually approaching it! But whatever its thoughts, once having looked away it could not make itself look back.

And all the time that Magnus continued to inch toward it, it crouched motionless, only the twitching of its tail, with anger one might have thought, making it appear even stiller. But it was not anger. It was fright.

And suddenly the watchers realized it.

"Don't go no further, my love!" cried Madeleine. "Stop where you be now. The nasty old cat's going to go away!"

"The better part of valor is discretion!" called Marcus Aurelius.

Roland alone had the wit to realize that this was the moment when the priceless shift in the balance of power brought about by Magnus's stoutheartedness must not be let go to waste. The enemy must not be allowed the luxury of a dignified withdrawal. All that would lead to would be a deadly ambush for the gallant young mouse at a later date. Magnus must strike home!

Though Roland was slow of speech and movement, his brain was quick; and through it flashed a number of courses he might take at this vital moment. He could explain ("Listen, lad, now's your chance, if you don't take it, you'll regret it later"—too lengthy). He could taunt ("Come on, lad, who's afraid of the big bad pussycat then?"—but Magnus patently was not). Or he could simply shout encouragement ("Get in there, lad! Have a go! Knock his block off!"). But before he could open his mouth, having decided upon this last approach, the matter was settled for him.

All at once the cat's nerve broke, for Magnus was now but a yard from it, and it rose and began to turn away. And as it swung round, lionlike no longer,

Magnus made his move. With a most un-Christian lack of love for his enemy and a great cry of "Bite you!" he sprang for the departing tail and once again fastened his jaws upon its ginger tip.

But how different was this from that first encounter! Five times as heavy, five times as strong, his long cutting teeth five times as sharp as on that other occasion, Magnus lay back and hauled like the anchorman in a tug-of-war team as the now terrified cat made desperately for home.

Scrabbling madly at the ground, it somehow managed to drag its fierce assailant into the fringe of the forest of Brussels sprouts, only for Magnus to wrap his own tail around the strong stem of a sprout plant, and take the strain. Something had to give!

Suddenly, with a bloodcurdling screech of pain, the cat broke free. But at what cost! For as it disappeared from their sight at speed, the watchers could see the spoils of victory hanging from Magnus's jaws.

Slowly he came toward them, out of the blood-flecked Brussels sprouts, and like the matador who offers to the ringsiders the ear of the vanquished bull, laid on the ground below the hutch an inch of ginger tail tip.

"Nasty!" said Magnus thoughtfully, cleaning his whiskers.

Above him there was pandemonium as the onlookers expressed their joy. " 'E beat 'im, 'e beat 'im, 'e beat that ole pussy!" squeaked Madeleine as she waltzed wildly around the floor in her excitement. As

49

for Marcus Aurelius, only Latin was good enough for this moment. "Victor ludorum!" he cried. "O Magnus magnificens, te salutamus!"

"What's all that mean then, Markie?" asked Madeleine.

"The Winner of the Games," explained Marcus. "O magnificent Magnus, we salute you!"

"I should think we does," said Madeleine.

But it was Roland who unwittingly provided the title by which Maddie and Markie's giant son was always to be known when future generations of mice spoke of his deeds.

"What a lad you've got there!" he boomed to the proud parents. "What size! What strength! Why, he's a positive powerhouse!"

"Power*mouse*, you means!" said Madeleine with a squeal of laughter.

And so Magnus Powermouse got his name.

CHAPTER 7

To the Potting Shed

When the cheering had died down and Magnus had scaled the table to be introduced to the rabbit ("Call me Uncle Roland, dear boy!"), it was plain to all that the wire mesh was far too small to allow him to enter the hutch. He could not even get his foot through it.

"Bite it!" said Magnus, and his excitement at the idea, coupled with his raging hunger, forced from him the longest speech of his young life. "Magnus make big hole!" he said. "Come inside Uncle Roland's house! Eat *all* food! Nice!"

Madeleine beamed with fatuous pride at these remarks, while Marcus Aurelius considered them critically.

"Such a course of action is undoubtedly possible," he observed. "Teeth sharp enough to cut through a cat's tail would make short work of this wire. Of that I have no doubt."

"Nor have I," said Roland. "But, I ask you, is it wise?"

"Wise?"

"Consider the situation. We are all dependent upon the humans for our livelihood, directly in my case, indirectly in yours. Imagine their feelings this morning when they see their cat. Their bobtailed cat. An accident, they may suppose. Or next door's dog. But if on top of that, they come down here—as they shortly will, to feed me—and find not just the evidence, lying down there on the ground, but a great hole cut in the front of my hutch, what do you suppose they will think?"

"They'll think something funny's been going on," said Madeleine absently.

"No, no, Maddie," said Marcus. "You do not see what Mr. Roland means. The humans will think that he is the culprit. All the evidence will then point to it."

"And they eat rabbits," said Roland quietly. "Don't forget that."

At the mention of eating, Magnus, who had not understood the conversation, set his teeth to the wire.

"No, Magnus!" cried Madeleine sharply. "Mummy says *no*!"

Surprise made Magnus let go, but this was quickly succeeded by another reaction. Never had he been crossed before, never denied or forbidden anything. He shouted angrily at his mother, "Nasty Mummy! Magnus want bite wire! Magnus want food!"

"Perhaps you should humor him, Maddie dear," said Marcus Aurelius uncertainly. "We don't want any unpleasantness."

"Unpleasantness?" cried Madeleine on a rising note. "Humor him? I'll give him what for if he don't do what he's told, that's what I'll do. You leave that wire alone, Magnus, and you get down off the table, this instant, d'you hear me, you naughty boy?"

There was a moment's silence and then, in very sulky tones, "Magnus bite Mummy," said the naughty boy.

At this Madeleine's control broke. Doting mother she might be, upon this child more than upon all her many previous children, but there were limits. She had been brought up to respect her elders and betters and only to speak when spoken to. "Children should be seen and not heard"—even now she could hear the acid voice of an old maiden aunt laying down this law.

Furiously she shot through the wire and fastened her needle teeth in the tip of her son's large snout. There followed a squeak of pain, a scrabbling of claws as Magnus tried to keep his balance on the edge of the table upon which the hutch stood, and then a loud thump as he hit the ground below.

"Serves you right," called Madeleine. She turned to Marcus Aurelius. " 'Tis all your fault, Markie," she said. "You should have been firmer with him when he were little." And she ran down the table leg.

Roland's nose twitched madly at the expression on Marcus's face. "A very determined lady," he said in his deep tones. Marcus made no reply, so he went on, "However, we have not solved the problem of feeding the lad, have we?"

Marcus Aurelius still made no answer. His feelings, usually so controlled, were in a terrible muddle. As well as the fear which never left him when outside the safety of his den, he felt still the pride at Magnus's victory over the cat mixed up with the disapproval of his son's insolence and the shame of being told off (and most unfairly told off, he said to himself) by his wife in front of this distinguished new friend.

All of this Roland sensed. Below them they could hear Magnus saying plaintively, "Mummy hurt nose," and Madeleine dealing with the matter as mothers do—"You should have done what Mummy told you. Mummy knows best. There, there, don't cry, Mummy will kiss it better."

Roland turned carefully toward Marcus Aurelius, his long ears dragging on the hutch floor with a soft slurring noise.

"Women are good at those sorts of things, aren't they, old chap?" he said in a man-to-man voice. "But it's the breadwinners who really matter, eh? Now, as head of the family, no doubt your prime concern is to solve the question of an adequate food supply for your boy?"

"Yes," said Marcus.

"And obviously you have worked out, clever fellow that you are, that there's a store of this mixture that they feed me, somewhere about the place?"

"Yes," said Marcus.

"You're a sharp one. I can see that you know where it's kept."

Marcus tried hard to look knowing.

"My word, yes," said Roland. "I should have realized that a chap of your intelligence would have known where it was."

"You mean," said Marcus hopefully, "in the . . . ?"

"Exactly," said Roland. "So if I were you, I'd pop down to that excellent little wife of yours and tell her to stop worrying because you've got it all worked out. Be masterful, y'know. But what am I saying? Anyone can see that you're the master in your own house."

"Yes," said Marcus.

"Or, for that matter, in the potting shed," said Roland quietly, his nose twitching.

"Ah," said Marcus Aurelius. "Exactly," he said. "As a matter of fact, I was just on my way there."

Madeleine was amazed, to say the least of it, when Marcus Aurelius came shinning down the table leg and snapped at her in a sharp voice of command.

"Follow me!" he said. "On the double."

"Crumbs!" said Madeleine to herself. "Whatever's come over the old chap? Hope he knows where he's going—he's as blind as a bat."

She was turning to obey her lord and master when a thought struck her. "Magnus," she said, "pick up that old cat's tail and fling it over into next door's garden, and then come on after us." Let someone else get the blame, she thought.

She ran on after Marcus. "Where are we going, Markie?" she panted as she drew level.

"To the potting shed!" cried Marcus Aurelius confidently.

The potting shed was in the far corner of the cottage garden, diagonally opposite the pigsty, and much too far away from either their summer or winter homes for the mice ever to have visited. Madeleine however knew whereabouts it was, and she was reasonably certain that her husband did not. Something told her not to upset his newfound confidence by criticism, so she ranged level with him and by tactfully shouldering him round as they ran got him pointing in the right direction. Behind them they heard the ground-shaking thunder of feet as Magnus caught up with them.

When they reached the open door of the shed, Marcus Aurelius stopped and faced his wife and child. A Moses among mice, he had led his people to the Promised Land, and he wanted the moment to have its full dramatic effect.

"Here," cried Marcus Aurelius, "is plenty!" and he climbed upon a stack of boxes and thus onto a shelf. Upon it, his nose told him—for his eyes were too weak—was the supply of rabbit food. What his nose did not tell him about was the danger that lay between him and that splendid-smelling brown paper bag toward which he rashly bounded. Madeleine saw it but too late.

"Markie!" she cried in horror. "Look out! Mind the—" but her words were cut off by that awful sound that comes as a death-knell to many a mouse.

"*Snap!*" went the trap.

CHAPTER 8

Daddy Means "Thank You"

All his life Magnus remembered the noise his father made in the trap. It was the more horrible to hear, the more awful to recall, because it was a very small noise.

Marcus Aurelius, running blindly for the bag of rabbit food, had stepped upon the very edge of one corner of the pan, and the cruel metal arm, springing shut with the speed of light, caught him by the toes of one hind foot.

"Oh! Oh!" cried Marcus Aurelius quietly. "Oh! Oh! Oh!"

Beside him Madeleine was frantic with distress at the sight and sound of her husband's agony.

"Markie! Markie!" she whispered through chattering teeth. "What shall us do?"

No mouse, she knew, ever got out of a mousetrap. Even those who avoided the usual broken neck, and were held as tortured prisoners by tails or ears or legs, must die, of shock, or pain, or starvation. And anyway, finally, the humans would come.

Even as she thought this, she saw through the open door of the potting shed the man come out of his cottage and start across the lawn toward them, a little bucket swinging in his hand.

If only she were strong enough to lift the spring
arm and release the wretched captive! But it would
need a mouse of giant strength to do such a thing,
she thought. A mouse with jaws of tremendous power,
she thought. "A powermouse!" she cried. "Of course!
Of course! Magnus, come quickly—there's no time
to waste!" For already the man was halfway to them.

Magnus blundered forward and licked his moaning father's nose in sympathy, half drowning him in the process. He sniffed the sprung trap.

"What this?" he said.

"It's a mousetrap," said Madeleine.

"Nasty."

"Of course it's nasty, you silly boy! Save your breath and get Daddy out of it."

"How do that?"

"Grab ahold of this arm with your teeth, here, see, and lift it."

Magnus gripped in his mouth the metal of the spring arm, held a fraction of an inch above the wooden pan by Marcus's toes, and lifted. Trap, and trapped mouse dangling from it, flew up into the air.

"Oh! Oh!" said Marcus Aurelius weakly.

"No! No!" said Madeleine. "Stand the other way around, Magnus. Put your feet on the pan, here, see, to hold it down while you pulls."

Magnus turned and stood upon the trap and took a fresh grip on the spring arm. He strained backward with all his might, but the spring was very strong and it seemed that he would not be able to move it.

Half mad with worry, for now she could hear the man's footsteps outside, Madeleine screamed furiously at her son. "Harder! Try harder, Magnus!" she screeched. "Or I'll bite your nose again!" And at this threat Magnus jerked his head back and the spring arm rose. Only a fraction did it move, but it was enough for Marcus Aurelius to pull his foot away.

"Quick, quick!" hissed Madeleine. "Behind these flowerpots, the pair of you." And when the man entered the shed there wasn't a mouse to be seen. He picked up the bag of rabbit food and poured some into his little bucket. His mind on other things, he did not notice the sprung trap, which lay where Magnus had dropped it, the marks of his teeth upon its rusty arm and upon its wooden pan a dark drying spatter of little blood drops.

When the man's footsteps had died away, they all came out of their hiding place. Magnus made straight for the rabbit food. He slashed the paper bag open so that a thick brown river of the stuff ran out over the shelf, and he fell upon it, jaws champing rhythmically.

Marcus Aurelius limped painfully out from behind the flowerpots, supported by an anxious Madeleine.

"Oh, Markie, Markie, your toes is all broken," she whispered.

"My toes *are* all broken," said Marcus automatically.

"Yes, yes, I know, dear. Does it hurt very bad?"

"*Badly*, Maddie. Yes, very badly." He paused. "Very badly indeed," he said.

"Try a bit to eat, dear," said Madeleine gently, "while I cleans your poor foot up," and she set to licking the injured part.

"Come on, Daddy," said Magnus with his mouth full. "Nice grub. Make Daddy better."

By the end of the morning things were looking up.

Marcus Aurelius's foot was still very painful (it was to leave him with a limp for the rest of his life) but a good meal and the tender ministrations of his wife had combined to restore him to something like his old wordiness. The guilt which he felt at having spoken scathingly of his son to Roland, added to genuine gratitude, led him to deliver a short formal speech.

"Magnus my boy," he said, "I have to thank you, from, I may add, the bottom of my heart, for your remarkable feat of strength in releasing me from that . . . object." He could not bring himself to say "trap." "But for you I should undoubtedly have experienced that cure of all diseases, that pale cold state that makes equal the high mouse and the low, that closes all, that cometh soon or late, that taketh all away. Pray accept my gratitude, dear boy. My undying gratitude, I may truthfully say."

Magnus looked puzzled.

"Daddy means 'thank you,' " said Madeleine.

She looked fondly upon her loved ones. Her husband was in pain, certainly, but alive, in his right mind, saved from a horrid fate! And his savior, that powermouse of a son of theirs, his mighty jaws still working, his great stomach happily distended—what a giant among mice was he! "A most honorable condition," that nice Mr. Roland had said. Everything in the garden was lovely.

But immediately, such was her nature, Madeleine began to worry. Marcus Aurelius would need nursing, careful nursing. But where? He would not be able to forage for himself for some time. He would need to be close to a good supply of food.

Should they go back into the cottage? No, Magnus could not, and though Marcus would be warm in his den, it would be such a business carrying all his food to him along those long corridors behind the wainscot, food that would be hard to get, too.

Should they stay here in the potting shed? Magnus perhaps. Plenty of grub here, and Magnus with his youth and his strength and his thick coat would not mind the cold; but it would not do for Marcus. He must have warmth and comfortable lying. Back to the pigsty? But it would not provide these necessities.

Madeleine was not normally at a loss in the making of commonsense decisions. She did not like to bother Marcus Aurelius for his opinion, especially since he was now dozing uneasily, his injured foot stuck stiffly out from his side. She looked across at Magnus.

Suddenly, perhaps because of his deeds that day,

he seemed no longer a baby but a fully grown mouse. Or at least I hopes he's fully grown, she thought. For the first time, she sought his advice.

"Magnus," said Madeleine. "Where'd be the best place for Daddy to go, to rest up comfy, warm, with plenty to eat, till he's better?"

"Gunk Roll," said Magnus without looking up.

Instantly Madeleine changed back into her role of disciplinarian.

"How dare you speak to me with your mouth full?" she snapped. "You ever do that again, I'll box your ears!"

Magnus backed hastily away and swallowed.

"Go to Uncle Roland," he said. "He nice. Safe place, no cat, no trap. Plenty grub. Daddy like."

Madeleine considered. She was sure the rabbit would offer them sanctuary. They could snuggle up to him for warmth, food and water would be on hand. But the journey there would be terribly slow, Marcus Aurelius hobbling, an easy prey.

"Go in dark," said Magnus as though reading her thoughts.

"But the owls . . ."

"Bite you owl!" cried Magnus cheerfully.

"But where will you go?"

"Come back here. Plenty place hide. Good grub."

And so it fell out. When night came, they made their way out of the potting shed and back across to the rabbit hutch, Marcus painfully on three legs, Madeleine anxiously, her eyes searching the darkness, her nose aquiver, Magnus confidently, his heavy muzzle swinging from side to side as he cast about for something nasty to bite.

By moonrise all was quiet. In the hutch the two little mice lay fast asleep, one under each of Roland's huge lop ears, which covered them like the most luxurious velvety white blankets.

Magnus had returned to the potting shed, and the noise of eating had resumed. When the man entered it the following morning carrying his little bucket, he stopped in the doorway and his mouth fell open. On the shelf was the brown paper bag that had contained quite a quantity of rabbit food. It was empty. Then he noticed the trap. He picked it up and saw upon the rusty metal of the spring arm the bright marks of Magnus's mighty teeth.

"Rats!" he said out loud. "Must be. A plague of them, I should think," and he hurried back across the lawn to telephone the ratcatcher.

CHAPTER 9

Jim the Rat

The ratcatcher was a well-known figure in the cottages and farms of the village and of the neighborhood. He was one of those people who seem always to have been around. He dealt also with mice of course, and moles, and anything else that he considered to be vermin, but his chief interest was revealed in his name.

Nobody, not even the smallest children, called him Mr. Johnson. To everyone, he was Jim to his face. But behind his back, he was always known as Jim the Rat.

Jim the Rat was short and fat, his eyes were the color of the bottom of a duck pond and he was bald.

When he arrived later that morning in a noisy old van, Magnus was asleep inside an old boot in which he had passed the night. (The potting shed contained a number of old boots, all right-footed. The cottager always seemed to get holes in his left boots but he kept the old rights, hoping his luck would change.)

At the sound of human voices Magnus awoke. He debated whether to shout "Nasty!" or "Bite you!" but something told him to remain silent.

"I should say there was at least a couple of pounds of rabbit food left yesterday," the cottager was saying as the two men came into the shed. "And it's all gone

this morning, Jim, every scrap of it. Take an army of
rats to eat that lot so quick—place must be running
with them."

Jim the Rat took a large red white-spotted handkerchief out of his pocket and blew his nose, very
carefully.

Jim the Rat's nose was short and squashy, with big
nostrils pointing straight ahead, like a pig's. He low-
ered it now to the shelf and sniffed deeply.

"No rats here," he said.

"How can you tell?"

"Can't smell 'em."

"What can you smell then?"

"Mice."

"You can tell the difference then?"

"Tell 'em all apart—rat, mouse, vole, shrew. Tell the different sorts of mice apart—house mouse, field mouse, harvest mouse. Good nose I've got."

"Well, what in the world's been eating my rabbit mixture then?"

"House mouse."

"Oh, come on, Jim! Polish off two pounds of the stuff in twenty-four hours? And have a look at this trap. See these tooth marks?"

Jim the Rat picked up the trap and put it to his nose. "House mouse," he said again. He looked at the empty brown paper bag, noticing how it was torn open. He looked under the shelf, at a litter of old seed boxes and sacks and four right-footed boots, one lying on its side. His piggy nostrils flared.

"Puzzle," said Jim the Rat. "You'll have to get some more food for the old rabbit then?" he said.

"That's right. Going down the shop shortly."

"Well, put it somewhere else. Not in here. Put it in a tin, a good strong tin. And another thing. Don't come in here at all for a few days, all right? Anything you need from this shed, take it out now. Can you manage that?"

"What are you up to then, Jim? Going to poison 'em?"

"No, but keep the cat away. Shut the door."

"That reminds me," said the cottager. "That blasted dog next door, took the end of our Tibby's tail off. It's lying there on the other side of the fence."

Jim the Rat's duck-pond eyes narrowed, and he looked again at the tooth marks on the trap. "Ah," he said. "Well, I expect you'll be wanting to get off down the shop. Don't bother waiting about for me, I'll be a while yet. You just keep this door shut and I'll look in tomorrow, all right?"

Jim the Rat waited until the cottager had mounted his bicycle and pedaled away down the lane, and then he fetched a trap from his van. No ordinary trap was this, but the strongest catch'em-alive contraption that he owned. It was the size of a large apple box and made of metal and heavy-gauge crisscrossed wire. He used it along the river banks, to catch coypu and mink that had gone wild. He put it on the potting shed shelf. To bait it he normally used a piece of meat, for mink, and for coypu some root vegetable such as carrot or beetroot.

"Something special for you though, I think, my friend," said Jim the Rat, and he took from his pocket what was to have been his midmorning snack, a Mars Bar. He unwrapped it, placed it carefully within, and set the trap. He went out quietly and shut the door.

"I wonder," said Jim the Rat out loud, as he drove his noisy old van away down the lane, "I wonder," and his piggy eyes gleamed.

All his rat-catching life he had been fascinated by a legend, a legend not perhaps as well-known as that of the Loch Ness Monster or the Abominable Snow-man, but to him, because of his profession, more interesting. It was the legend of the King Rat.

Jim the Rat had read everything he could lay his hands on about this creature of folklore, stories from many different lands and of many different times. All of them told of one thing in common. In any gathering of rats, especially a large gathering such as might occur in war or plague, or in sewers, or in deserted places whence humans had fled before some catastrophe, there would always be one mighty leader, the King Rat. A giant he was, a huge brute before whom cats would quail and dogs run yelping. Some of the tales told of humans attacked by an army of squeaking chattering rats, the King at their head. Often this was at night, where a foolhardy man might perhaps have been exploring a cellar, in a ruined town. By the light he carried, a flaring torch maybe, he would suddenly see, even before a sound was heard, a thousand glistening eyes in the darkness and before them a single pair far larger than the rest. But would he live to tell the tale?

And, just as many people believe in the Loch Ness Monster or the Great Sea Serpent or Bigfoot, so Jim Johnson believed in the existence of King Rats. He had no proof, it is true. He had killed some big old rats in his time, but they were just big old rats. But he was always on the lookout for something unusual as he went about his business. And this morning he had found it!

It was not just the amount of food that had gone, not just the tooth marks on the trap. His sharp eyes had seen muddy footmarks on the paper sacks underneath the potting-shed shelf. They were very large footmarks, bigger than the average rat's.

There was no King Rat in that potting shed, but there was something very big, something that his good nose told him of, unmistakably.

"I wonder," said Jim the Rat softly. "Could it be a King Mouse?"

Magnus, meantime, had drifted back to sleep. He had listened to the men's voices, and to various noises ending in the shutting of the door. It passed through his mind, a mind made more than usually slow by the amount of food he had eaten, that he was now a prisoner, but he was warm and comfortable in the old boot and he could always bite his way out of the shed when he wanted to.

He woke again when his ears told him of noise and his nose of a particularly delicious smell. He climbed out of the boot and up onto the shelf, and his eyes showed him a scene of revelry.

Half a dozen mice were nibbling eagerly at the dark-brown object from which the lovely smell came. They were squeaking with excitement and joy, and at first they did not notice Magnus. Then one suddenly said, "Look out, boys! Rat coming!" and they all stopped eating and stared.

"Not rat," said Magnus in a rather hurt voice.

70

"What are you then?" said another.

Magnus hesitated, a little shy with these shrill strangers, and a third one said cheekily, "Lost your tongue then?"

Magnus felt himself growing angry. "Me mouse," he said gruffly.

At that they all fell about, squeaking with helpless mirth. "Me mouse, me mouse, me mouse!" they screamed, until, tiring of the joke, they turned their backs on him and fell to nibbling again.

Magnus saw red. One end of the metal contraption in which the mice were feasting was open, he could see, and in through this he dashed with a thundering cry of "Bite you!" so loud as to drown the click of the trap door closing behind him as his weight set it off.

He found himself alone, for the others had vanished through the wire mesh, and in front of him the sweet-smelling object, hardly marked by the tiny teeth that had so far attacked it. Eagerly, effortlessly, Magnus Powermouse picked up the Mars Bar. Holding it in his forepaws, he opened wide his mouth and bit off a large lump.

"Nice!" said Magnus, and took another great bite. "Nice!" he said again. By midday the Mars Bar was finished.

"More!" said Magnus mechanically.

He looked around for the other mice but there was no sign of them. He looked for the door through which he had entered but there was no sign of it. He butted at each side of the metal box but each side was unyielding. He tried the heavy wires with his teeth but all to no avail. And as he rested a moment, panting with fury and frustration, Madeleine's words came clearly to his mind from those far-off lessons in the pigsty. "Beware thou the trap!"—he could remember the exact pitch and tone of them now, spoken in that voice he loved so well, that voice that he would never hear again!

At that instant, the day's strong wind, blowing across the garden from the north, brought upon it the scent of his beloved mother.

He threw back his head.

"MUMM-YYY!" cried Magnus Powermouse.

CHAPTER 10

The Seventh Buck

The day's strong wind, blowing across the garden from the north, completely drowned Magnus's cries for help. Madeleine for once was not actually thinking about her son, so busy was she fussing around her injured husband.

At the suggestion of "that nice Mr. Roland," she had made him up a comfortable bed of hay in the inner sleeping compartment of the hutch, hidden from passersby. She busied herself carrying him the choicest pieces from the rabbit's food bowl (Marcus Aurelius particularly fancied the flaked maize).

Roland watched her comings and goings with affection. A lonely old bachelor, he had learned to put up with solitude, and only now did he realize how much he had missed the company of others. He found himself very much drawn to this family of mice: Madeleine with her shrewd country sense, sharp tongue and soft heart, the educated long-winded Marcus Aurelius and that extraordinary boy of theirs.

Madeleine paused in her work and made a sort of little bob in front of him.

"Oh, I don't know what you must think of me, Mr. Roland," she said, "treating this house of yours

as though it was me own, and us eating all your food and I don't know what!"

"My dear lady," said Roland in his deep tones, "I am delighted to have you both. There can be no question of your leaving until your husband is fully restored. As for food, there is plenty. Mind you, it would be a different matter if we were catering for that son of yours! I wonder how he's getting on?"

"Oh, he'll be all right, he can look after hisself," said Madeleine, even as the north wind muffled Magnus's frantic yells.

By nightfall the wind had dropped and the yells had stopped. Because there was nothing else to do, Magnus sat in the trap and waited. He had shouted till his throat was sore, he had bitten at the wire till

74

his mouth was bleeding. He had even asked the potting-shed mice for help, but they of course could not open the catch that held the trap shut and he could not reach it. At last his rage changed to a sort of resignation, and he settled down to wait and see what morning would bring.

Morning brought Jim the Rat, very early. At the first peep of light, long before anyone was stirring, he slipped through the garden gate and along the edge of the lawn to the potting shed. He had left his van half a mile away. If the trap was empty, he could slip away again unnoticed. But he did not think it would be empty. Ordinary mice loved tiny bits of chocolate, he knew—he often used them as bait. So how would this one resist a king-sized Mars Bar? And about one thing Jim the Rat was certain. If he should be the first person—ever—to catch a King Mouse, he wanted no one to know of it. He opened the door.

At the sight of the man Magnus fluffed himself up until he looked even bigger, and with one loud shout of "Nasty! Bite you!" reared threateningly upon his hind legs as a hand came toward him. But the hand held a piece of cheese, which it thrust through the wire mesh and into the gaping mouth. With his other hand Jim the Rat grabbed a heavy sack and threw it over the cage; he picked it up and was gone, closing the shed door quietly behind him.

The morning was still, and in the rabbit hutch Magnus's shout had been plainly heard.

"Oh, crumbs!" cried Madeleine. "What's he up to

75

now?'' and she ran to the wire and peered out. Marcus Aurelius limped and Roland lolloped after her.

"I see a human," said Marcus Aurelius. "A human, moreover, of a physical type which might reasonably be described as corpulent."

"A fat man," said Roland softly in Madeleine's ear.

"He is moving," said Marcus Aurelius, "with the utmost prudence—"

"Carefully," whispered Roland.

"—and carrying an object—"

"Thing."

"—the contents of which are indiscernible."

"We don't know what's in it."

"I can see all that," snapped Madeleine. "What I wants to know is, is our Magnus in it?"

"I hardly think so," said Roland comfortingly. "I can hear nothing."

At that moment the reason for Magnus's silence ceased to exist, as he swallowed the last of the cheese, and the early morning air was rent by one great cry.

"More!!" yelled Magnus Powermouse from the darkness of the trap.

Then the garden gate clicked, and the footsteps of Jim the Rat died away down the lane.

In the hutch there was a long silence. Roland glanced sideways at the faces of his little friends, faces that suddenly looked pinched and old as they stared blankly out.

All his common sense (of which he had a great deal)

76

told him that this was the end of Magnus Power-mouse. All his kindliness (of which he had a great deal) told him to give no hint of this. He decided to pretend to an ability (of which he had none) to foresee the future. He cleared his throat impressively.

"Now, listen to me, you two," he said in his deep-est, most authoritative tones. "Everything's going to be all right."

"With all due respect, Mr. Roland," said Marcus Aurelius heavily, "I find that statement difficult to believe. We must be prepared to face facts. Magnus has been kidnapped."

"But what for, Markie?" said Madeleine in a shaking voice. "What d'you suppose that human wanted him for?"

"To eat, I daresay," said Marcus gloomily. "He likes his food, from the look of him." Madeleine gave a little squeak of horror.

"Now, now!" said Roland sharply. "That's quite enough of that sort of talk. Humans do not eat mice. They kill them, to be sure, but if that fat man had wished to kill your son, he could presumably easily have done so. He has not done so. Magnus is alive and well, as we heard. And so he will continue to be. You mark my words. I know."

"Know?" cried Madeleine with a return to something like her usual snappiness. "How can you know?"

"I have the gift."

"The gift?"

"Of looking into the future."

77

A gleam came into Marcus Aurelius's dull eyes. "Really?" he said. "The gift of divination! How extremely interesting! The ancient Greeks and Romans, you know, made—"

"Oh, bide quiet, Markie!" interrupted Madeleine. "We don't want to know about your old ancient folk. Tell us more, Mr. Roland—how come you can see into the future then?"

"Because I," said Roland, "am the seventh buck of a seventh buck."

"Crumbs!" whispered Madeleine.

"And I hereby solemnly tell you, Madeleine and Marcus Aurelius, that one day, someday, I cannot tell exactly when, you will see that noble giant of a son of yours again. I can see it all in my mind's eye—the triumphal reunion of Magnus Powermouse with his pretty little mother and his wise father." And his lying old uncle, he thought to himself. Here I am, rabbiting on about second sight when really I haven't a clue. But it was worth it, for the look on their faces. Let's just hope I'm right.

CHAPTER 11

Fit for a King

Jim Johnson lived alone. That is to say, he had no wife or family or any other human being to share his home. Yet it was full to overflowing—with animals.

For though the killing of vermin was his job, which he did cold-bloodedly and efficiently, Jim the Rat kept pets of all shapes and sizes. Some were useful to him, like the three cats that made sure he did not have to practice his trade on his own patch. Some earned their keep in other ways, like the two goats that provided his milk and the hens and ducks that laid his eggs. And some were creatures that had somehow landed up with him: guinea pigs that children had grown tired of, a tame jackdaw, a number of singing birds—canaries, linnets, and bullfinches—and an ancient donkey that lived in the little orchard and made terrible groaning creaking noises to show how happy it was.

In fact, when he wasn't killing them, Jim the Rat had a great way with animals of all sorts, and could never refuse the offer of another pet. Even the latest addition to his menagerie already felt this.

Magnus sat, silent for once, in the mink trap which had been placed on the kitchen table, and watched the short fat bald figure moving neatly and quickly around the crowded room. Soon he heard a sizzling noise, and then there came to his uplifted nose the most heavenly smell. For once he did not shout, but only murmured, "Nice. Nice. Me like," as the sausages browned and bubbled in the pan.

At the low noise Jim the Rat turned from the stove. As soon as he had reached home he had inspected Magnus from every angle, his duck-pond eyes shining with excitement as his suspicions were confirmed, for in every way, he saw clearly, this was a mouse. In every way, that is, except for one—its giant size. Indeed, indeed, he had captured a King Mouse! He addressed Magnus accordingly.

"What's up then, Your Majesty?" he said.

Magnus could not understand the rumbling voice, but something in him liked the sound of it.

"What you got?" he said. "Smell good. You give Magnus some? Magnus hungry."

Jim the Rat in his turn heard only a jumble of urgent throaty squeaks, but there was no mistaking the meaning of them. The way to the royal heart, he thought, is through the royal stomach, and he speared a sausage and held it close to the trap.

Magnus stood up to his full height, his feet upon the wire, his nose aquiver, whiskers twitching, pleading eyes almost bolting from his head.

"Nice man!" he said. "Nice grub! Magnus want bite!"

"Make a meal fit for a king," said Jim the Rat,

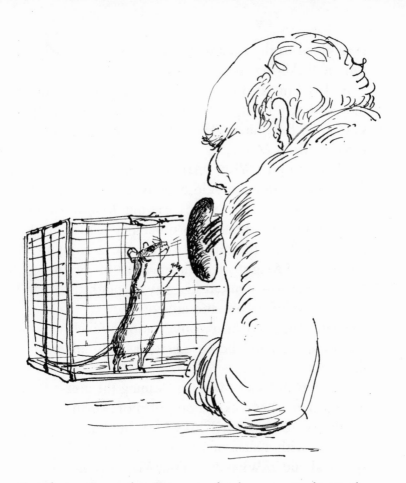

"pork sausages do. But we don't want to burn the royal mouth, Your Majesty, so you'll have to wait a minute," and he put the sausage on a plate to cool and turned away to see to e rest.

The old Magnus would have been ranting and raging by now at not having his wishes immediately granted, but already something in his association with the ratcatcher had changed him. He stayed quiet, his eyes glued to the source of that marvelous smell, his tongue flickering over his lips.

At last Jim sat down to his own breakfast, but he did not begin until he had tested the heat of the first sausage in his fingers. He cut off a piece and offered it to the King Mouse.

"May it please Your Majesty," he said.

The old Magnus would have bolted it and bawled for more, but the times were changing. Man and mouse ate steadily, watching each other the while and enjoying the food the more for the other's enjoyment. By the time Magnus had finished his bit of sausage, Jim the Rat had worked his way through three, and two rashers of bacon, and an egg.

They continued their conversation, which was no less companionable because neither could understand the other's tongue.

"Nice grub!" said Magnus, cleaning the grease from his whiskers. "Me like! You got more, man?"

"Pretty good was it?" asked Jim the Rat, mopping his plate with a slice of bread. "Meet with the royal approval, did it? What does Your Majesty fancy now?"

He cut another thick slice of bread from the loaf, cut off a finger from it about as long as his own and proffered it. Magnus drew it through the wire quite gently, and Jim allowed the tips of his finger and thumb to follow it in. As he had guessed, Magnus did not bite. Already the connection was made in his mind between nice things and nice man, so nice fingers and nice thumb.

"Good boy," said Jim, forgetting for a moment that this was not the way to address a king. He slapped butter and honey on the rest of the slice.

"Magnus want," said Magnus hastily, and pushed his dry bread back out for the same treatment.

By the end of breakfast a firm bond had been established between the pair. Jim took the day off from rat catching and by the end of it had taught Magnus to come to the wire of the trap when called.

That evening the cottager telephoned.

"You coming round soon, Jim? I've been keeping the shed door closed like you said."

"I've been. You can open it," Jim said. "I reckon I've solved your little problem." He winked at the watching Magnus.

"I told you it was rats, Jim, I knew it. That old nose of yours was wrong for once, eh?"

"Maybe."

"Well now, what do I owe you?"

"No, that's all right, don't bother," Jim said. He suddenly felt he did not want to take money for this unique and extraordinary new pet. He gazed fondly on Magnus. A ratcatcher may look at a King Mouse, he thought.

"Look, tell you what, Jim," the cottager said. "My missus says we ought to get rid of the old rabbit. Says it's his food the rats and mice come after. Be any good to you? You can have his hutch and all."

"Well, thanks."

"All right then, let's leave it like this. Next time you're by with the van, you pick him up. OK?"

"Thanks," said Jim the Rat. "Maybe you could go in with him, Your Majesty," he said as he put the phone down. "Be company for you. After all, you can't stay in that mink trap forever. But first I've got to get you really tame."

And so for the next several days Jim spent every minute that he could spare from his work in training the King Mouse.

For a reward of food, Magnus learned not only to come, but to sit and to stay on command. Smarties, Jim found, were a useful form of payment. To Magnus, they seemed like a heavenly variety of Porker Pill.

In fact, the training was a two-way affair, for a short sharp squeak would always persuade the soft-hearted Jim to hand over an extra Smartie. He could not of course know that the squeak was an order for "More!"

By the end of a week, Jim the Rat had nerved himself to do what he knew he must if his control over the King Mouse was to be proved. He took what precautions he could. First he cleared the kitchen of cats. Then he closed all the doors and windows, and armed himself with a new packet of Smarties. Then he opened the door of the trap.

CHAPTER 12

Nightmare

Jim need not have worried. Magnus had no desire to run away from someone who supplied such a wonderful variety of delicious things to eat.

Soon he began to go everywhere perched upon Jim's shoulder, even to travel with him in the van (though Jim was careful to hide him away when they met other humans; a food offering would always persuade Magnus into a box, away from curious eyes, or, at the end of the day, back into the safety of the mink trap).

But suddenly one night, something happened which completely altered the best-laid plans of mouse and man.

Everything at Jim the Rat's cottage was quiet. Upstairs, Jim snored. Outside in the orchard the donkey dozed and the goats snoozed, and in their houses the hens and the ducks slumbered soundly. Only the hunting cats stalked through the shadowy moonlight.

In the mink trap on the kitchen table Magnus Powermouse slept also, but fitfully. Maybe it was the fault of supper—Jim had been generous with his own toasted cheese, and there had been a square of chocolate for dessert—but tummy ache and nightmares invaded Magnus's rest. He dreamed that he was in the grip of some monstrous bird of prey, so real a dream that he could feel its cruel talons piercing his stomach, and he woke with a scream of "MUMM-YY!"

At that very moment, as chance would have it, there was a mouse on the table looking for scraps, a female mouse, a mouse of a warm brown color, a mouse that looked in the light of the dying fire very much like Madeleine.

"Mummy?" cried Magnus once again before his nose told him that of course it was not. The stranger vanished and he was wide awake. And all at once a great flood of homesickness swept over him. He pictured his parents, even now happily asleep with kind Uncle Roland, his parents to whom he had barely given a thought for many days, and he cried. He recalled how his little mother had toiled and slaved to find enough food for him when he was a baby, and he cried yet more. He saw his poor father cruelly caught by the foot and wept bitterly.

"All my fault!" howled Magnus in the mink trap. "All because Magnus was so greedy. Nasty, nasty Magnus!"

By morning he had reduced himself to a state of abject misery, convinced that he would never see his mother and father again. If indeed they were still alive. Probably they had already been trapped, or poisoned, or eaten by the cat, or had simply died of broken hearts. As he surely must. And soon!

The moment Jim the Rat came downstairs, he could see that something was very wrong. Magnus was hunched in a corner of the trap and did not even look up when Jim opened the door.

Usually he would be waiting eagerly for the first "Come" and "Sit," the first Smartie reward, and the first "Good boy," but now he took no notice whatsoever of any command and no interest in any food that was offered. Jim even produced that favorite, a Mars Bar, and waved it under Magnus's nose, but it might as well have been a block of wood.

Ordinarily by now Magnus would have been happily perched upon Jim's shoulder while the ratcatcher went through his early-morning routine—cats let in, hens and ducks let out, goats milked, greetings exchanged with donkey, everything fed—but this morning Jim had to do it alone.

He did not think to close the mink-trap door.

As he went about his chores Jim wondered what to do. If the King Mouse was really ill, he must call the vet. But that would give the game away, people would get to hear about such an extraordinary animal, it would be in the papers, on the TV, there would be no privacy, no peace. Oh, I'll leave it awhile, he thought, maybe it's just a tummy upset, not surprising really when you consider how much he eats. But when he came back into the kitchen, the mink trap was empty.

"Your Majesty!" cried Jim anxiously. "Where are you?" But there was no sound in reply. Only the songbirds in their cages piped and whistled. He looked

fearfully for the cats, but, curiously, they had all disappeared. He searched the room from top to bottom but found nothing. He ran outside, calling "Come! Come! Good boy!" but there was no sign. He can't have gone far, thought Jim the Rat.

In fact Magnus had gone quite a long way. He had walked out of the trap in a kind of daze of unhappiness, for all he could think of now was how to try to find his way back to his mother and father, whom he had deserted and left to some terrible fate or other. He had quite forgotten that he had been taken from them against his will. He was full of guilt, and of anger, against himself, against Fate, against anything that got in his way.

What got in his way was a large black cat.

All three of Jim's cats had been waiting for just such
an opportunity as this. For weeks now they had been
able to see, to smell and to hear Magnus. Now they
could give their other two senses a turn. Touch him!
And then taste him!

When Magnus first came out of his refuge, none of
them moved. They sat around the table slit-eyed, tail
tips twitching. Cattily, they began to talk amongst
themselves in soft spiteful voices.

" 'E's a big un, ain't 'e, Ginger?"

"Not scared of him, are you, Tibbles?"

"Don't talk so daft. I'll soon give 'ee what for."

"Who said you could have 'im? You leave 'im to
me-ow."

"No, to me-ow!"

The big black, the boss cat, settled the argument.
He suddenly moved forward until he sat below Magnus, directly blocking his line of flight to the open
back door. His claws were unleashed, every muscle

was tensed and his tail moved slowly from side to side in a wide arc. He raised his head and his pale eyes looked directly into the dark ones above.

"Blackie's going to take 'im then!" they said.

"Old Blackie'll 'ave 'im!"

"Don't be in too much of a hurry then, Blackie. Play around with 'im a bit! Let's see a bit of sport!"

Surprise, as any fighting soldier knows, is a very valuable weapon in battle, and what happened next took the black cat completely by surprise. At one instant he was crouched in all the glory of his strength, the very picture of a mighty hunter. At the next he was struck full in the face by the furious missile that was Magnus, and scratched and buffeted and knocked off balance. Yowling with fright and hurt pride and a badly bitten ear, he dashed beneath the kitchen cabinet for shelter.

Rooted to the spot, Ginger and Tibbles watched the giant mouse dash out through the back door, while under the dresser Blackie mewed like a cuffed kitten.

CHAPTER 13

I'll Be Jugged!

In years to come the story of the battle in Jim the
Rat's kitchen grew to epic proportions. The great
Magnus Powermouse had taken on ten, twenty cats,
mouse mothers told their children. He had put them
all to flight, killing many, severely wounding others,
sparing none. ("Mind you don't try anything like that,
dear. You're only little, and he was a giant among
mice.")

But just at the moment the giant among mice was
at a loss. The blind fury which had prompted his
fearless attack upon the cat had worn off, and suddenly
he realized, as he ran headlong away from Jim's cottage, that although he was now determined to find
his parents, he did not know the way.

He stopped in the middle of a large field and tested
the wind with upraised snout but to no avail. He stood
upon his hind legs and gazed around, but even to a
giant mouse the view ended at the next hedge. He
threw back his head and yelled at the top of his voice.
"MUMM-YYY!! DADD-YYY!!" yelled Magnus to the skies
above, but there was no answer save for the whistle
of the wind.

After a moment however he heard the thump of
feet and saw a strange animal coming across the field

toward him. It leaped and twirled and turned som-
ersaults and chased its own tail, all at the highest speed;
and when it eventually reached Magnus, it took no
notice of him, but stood upon its hind legs and with
its forefeet wildly punched the air.

"Left!" and "Right!" cried the animal. "Jab! Jab!
Use your jab! Now get away and use your left! Draw
him! Now the counterpunch! Right cross to the jaw!
And an uppercut to finish him!" And it dropped down
on all fours, puffing and panting.

Magnus had never seen a hare before and did not
know that the month was March when all hares are

mad. However, it bore some vague resemblance to Uncle Roland and so might presumably be kindly. He decided to ask it the way to go.

"Which way Mummy and Daddy?" said Magnus politely.

The hare turned its head slightly. Its large mad eyes were set on the side of its head, so that it could not see comfortably when pointing its nose at him.

"Hey! A king-sized mouse! Fan-tastic! What did you say, boy?" it said, and it shot suddenly up in the air like a jack-in-the-box and landed facing in the other direction. Magnus repeated his question.

"Mummy and Daddy are dead and gone," it said in a singsong voice.

> *"Clamped in the long dogs' jaws*
> *Or killed by the hounds of the beagling folk*
> *Who hang up their masks and paws*
> *Or caught in the mesh of the poacher's net*
> *Or filled with the sportsman's lead.*
> *Don't know how, but I tell you now,*
> *Mummy and Daddy are dead."*

It stood upright and began boxing again.

"My mummy and daddy?" cried Magnus in an agony. "Dead?"

"No, not your mummy and daddy, stupid—Duck! Feint! Left jab! Now, hook him with your right!— *My* mummy and daddy."

"But which way *my* mummy and daddy?" said Magnus.

"Look, boy," said the hare. "How should I know? You might as well ask me where my Aunt Fanny is."

"Where your Aunt Fanny?" said Magnus obediently.

The hare looked sideways at him for a moment. Then it shook its head so that its very long ears wobbled wildly.

"Crazy boy," it said reflectively. "What's your name?"

"Magnus."

"Well how'd you like to go a couple of rounds with me, Magnus? Come on, boy, put up your dukes." It stood up on its hind legs once again and began to dance around Magnus, battering the air above his head with a perfect flurry of blows.

Eventually, since this display provoked no reaction but bewilderment, it dropped down and began to graze.

"What's dukes?" said Magnus.

With a sigh, the hare swallowed a mouthful of grass. "Dukes, Magnus," it said, "are the things on the end of your arms. Fists. Used in fisticuffs. Boxing. You like me to teach you how to, boy?"

"How to what?"

"Box."

"You put Magnus in box?"

"Magnus," said the hare in a tone of patient weariness, "you and I operate on different intellectual planes."

"Don't understand."

"Exactly. Now listen, crazy boy, and I'll try to explain to you about the noble art of self-defense," said the hare, and he rose upright once again and struck an attitude, advancing one hind foot and holding one forepaw up before his face, the other being tucked defensively against his chin. His mad eyes smoldered, and he cried out in ringing tones:

"If you can stand and fight with any fellow
And take a punch and hand one out as well,
If you can show you're true blue and not yellow
And keep your end up till the final bell;

"If you can brave the clouting and the clinching
And battle on until the fight is won,
If you can face the onslaught without flinching
Or giving ground—you'll be a Hare, my son!"

Magnus furrowed his brow. "Not hare, mouse," he said.

There was a long pause.

"Well, I'll be . . . jugged!" said the hare, and away he went across the field in a series of great sailing bounds until he was lost to sight.

Left alone, Magnus Powermouse was conscious of a number of different feelings. Puzzlement—for he had hardly understood a word the strange creature had said. Hunger—for he had never in his life been so long without food. And following on from that, regret—for here, in this windy field, there was no Jim the Rat, no Smarties, no bread and honey, no sausages, no Mars Bars. Not only did his mouth water at this last thought, but his eyes too, and for an instant he felt very lost. But then his courage reasserted itself.

Find Mummy and Daddy. That was what he had set out to do. That was what he was going to do.

At that very moment he heard in the distance a noise, a noise that he now knew well, the noise of a car engine. Motorcars needed roads, he reasoned, all roads went somewhere, he would find this road and follow it. He set off at a run.

CHAPTER 14

A Scream of Brakes

By the time Magnus reached the lane, Jim the Rat's van had disappeared round the next corner on its way to the very place that Magnus himself was seeking.

Jim had searched every corner of his own property unavailingly. I suppose he might have tried to get back home, he thought. I might come across him on the way perhaps. At the very least I can pick up that rabbit they offered me. Make a nice pet. Take my mind off His Majesty perhaps.

But he knew that it wouldn't. He was already missing the King Mouse very badly.

Magnus turned to follow the direction that the van had taken as soon as he hit the lane. He did not know which was the right way to go, he did not know that the vehicle had been Jim's van, he did not know why he made that choice, he just made it, in his usual direct fashion. And in his usual direct fashion, he set off walking in the middle of the road.

He plodded resolutely forward, his mind now empty of all thoughts save two. Magnus not see Mummy and Daddy, so Magnus unhappy. Mummy and Daddy not see Magnus, so Mummy and Daddy unhappy.

In fact a firm belief in Roland's gift of second sight had kept Madeleine perfectly happy.

From the start she had found something very reassuring about the great white rabbit with his deep comforting voice and his kindly red eyes and those huge soft floppy ears under which she and Marcus Aurelius slept so warmly every night. And to be told by him, solemnly, certainly, that they would all be reunited—well, that was it, then! No need to worry, everything in the garden was lovely!

Marcus Aurelius on the other hand was by no means as confident of ever seeing his son again, that son of whom he had suddenly grown very fond, so he spent much of his convalescence thinking of him. More skeptical by nature than his simple wife, he could not forget the facts of the matter, whatever Roland had said. Magnus had been captured by a human, and humans kill mice. The answer was obvious. All that remained was to write "Quod erat demonstrandum" after it.

"Q.E.D." said Marcus Aurelius sadly as he peered shortsightedly out of the rabbit hutch at the morning sunshine, some weeks after Magnus's disappearance.

"Q.E.D.? What's that mean, Markie?" asked Madeleine, emerging from beneath Roland's left ear.

"Er . . . quite an exquisite day, Maddie dear," said Marcus hastily.

"Funny way to talk," said Madeleine. She giggled. "B.S.I.O.W.W.T.S.O.M." she said.

"I beg your pardon?"

"Better still if only we was to see our Magnus."

"If only we *were* to see our Magnus."

"That's what I just said."

"Ah. Maddie my love, I pray you may never fall victim to groundless optimism."

"I hope I never does. Sounds horrible."

"What I mean, my love, is . . . do not set your heart upon seeing our boy again. Nothing is certain in this life."

"But my heart is set on it, Markie. And it is certain we shall see him. Uncle Roland said so."

Roland had been embarrassed by the way the mice addressed him, Marcus Aurelius as "Sir," Madeleine as "Mr. Roland." He could not persuade them to use his first name alone, so had eventually settled for "Uncle," a title with which they appeared comfortable.

At the sound of his name he hopped forward and squatted carefully between his two small friends.

"You did, didn't you?" said Madeleine.

"Did what, my dear Madeleine?" asked Roland.

"Say we should see Magnus again. That we should all be reunited."

"I did indeed."

"What interval of time," said Marcus Aurelius, "would you estimate must elapse before this happy vision might become reality?" For the life of him he could not keep a note of sarcasm out of his voice.

"He means how long before we sees him," translated Madeleine, and she could not keep the excitement from hers.

"Oh, I do not know exactly. . . ."

"Soon?"

"I sincerely hope so," said Roland. He crossed his paws.

At that very instant there was the sound of a motor coming up the lane. It stopped, the garden gate clicked, and there were footsteps on the gravel of the path. Roland, standing up against the wire door of his hutch, saw the approaching human before the mice. It was the fat man who had taken Magnus.

"Cave hominem!" snapped Roland. Marcus had taught him this Latin warning to "beware of the man," and at the sound of it, the mice would dart into the sleeping compartment and hide beneath the hay.

Outside they could hear the rumble of men's voices, fading for a few moments (for Jim had manufactured an excuse to have a look in the potting shed, hoping against hope) and then strengthening as they returned toward the hutch (Jim's duck-pond eyes darting everywhere, vainly seeking that familiar figure).

"Well, here's the old rabbit then, Jim," said the cottager. "You'll give him a good home, I know."

Madeleine and Marcus Aurelius cowered lower in the hay as the wire door of the hutch was opened. Then Roland felt strong fingers that yet were very gentle as they stroked the arch of his back, rubbed at the roots of his great ears, and finally smoothed the ears themselves, one at a time, softly, tenderly. He shivered with pleasure at the touch.

"He's a beauty," said Jim the Rat.

"Right then. Grab ahold of the other end of the hutch. I'll give you a lift into the van with it."

"Markie, Markie!" whispered Madeleine in terror as the old van went racketing off down the lane. " 'Tis the end of the world!"

"Courage, Maddie dear," said Marcus Aurelius through chattering teeth.

"All shall be well," said Roland, thrusting in his head from the outer compartment of the hutch. "Only stay hidden till I give the word."

The bumping and the rattling continued, accompanied by violent lurches as they swung round one of the many bends in the twisting road. Then suddenly, after one such lurch, the travelers in the hutch were thrown about as, with a scream of brakes, the van came to a shuddering halt.

The silence that followed was broken by the voice of Jim the Rat, a voice that suddenly sounded old and choked.

"Oh, no!" said Jim. "Oh, I never saw you, coming round that bend! Oh, Your Majesty, Your Majesty, what have I done?"

CHAPTER 15

Squash You Flat!

Fortunately for Magnus, there was no traffic about when he first reached the road. For one thing it was early, and for another it happened to be a Sunday. Anyway the twisty lane didn't really lead to anywhere much except Jim's cottage and a couple of farms. He pressed on therefore on the crest of the road surface, in the gravest danger from any vehicle which might come along. Though he was quite unaware of the risks he was running, someone else was not, for he soon heard a voice that he recognized.

"Crazy boy," said the hare, hopping along on the other side of the fence and staring sideways at him with its huge mad eyes, "get off the road."

Magnus increased his pace. "Going to find Mummy and Daddy," he said.

"You'll never make it, crazy boy," said the hare, lollopping easily in the field beside. "You want to know why?"

"No," said Magnus firmly. He broke into a gallop, but he could not escape the remorseless voice of his escort.

"Then I'll tell you," said the hare, and he began to intone:

"Mouse or hedgehog or stoat or rat
  Go on the road and they'll squash you flat!
  Snake or lizard or frog or toad
  They'll squash you flat if you go on the
    road!"

again and again and again, until Magnus's mind began
to spin at the relentless chanting and he ran even faster
in his efforts to be free of it.

"Squash you flat . . . squash you flat . . . squash you flat . . ." went over and over in his brain so that he heard nothing of the van as it swung round the sharp corner. Then there was only pain, and blackness, and silence.

For a moment Jim the Rat could not force himself to get out of his van and look. I've squashed him flat, he thought in horror. When he did get out, a movement caught his eye in the field beside the lane, but it was only a hare which ran away in a series of great leaps and buckjumps, stopping every now and then to stand upon its hind legs and shadowbox furiously with an imaginary opponent.

Beneath and behind the van, the surface of the road was empty. Feverishly, Jim the Rat began to search amongst the tangle of weeds and brambles by the side of the road.

Inside, the travelers conversed in nervous whispers.

"Oh, Markie, Markie, what's happened?"

"A minor catastrophe, I imagine."

"Oh, Uncle Roland, what's he mean?"

"There's been a small accident."

Then they heard the driver's door open again. There was the rumble of the man's voice—"Thank goodness . . . he's breathing . . . can't see anything broken . . . no blood . . . must have caught him a glancing blow . . . let's get home quick"—and then the sound of the engine starting.

As soon as Jim the Rat reached his cottage he carried

Magnus carefully inside. He put a cushion on the kitchen table and laid the unconscious King Mouse tenderly upon it. He ran back out to the van and picked up the rabbit hutch. Because he was anxious to get back to Magnus, he brought it into the kitchen and dumped it on the table. At the sight of the figure on the cushion Roland's red eyes positively bulged.

"Got to bring him round," said Jim the Rat, "but how? I know! Smelling salts! That's what Mother used to use when Grandma felt faint . . . little dark-blue bottle . . . got it somewhere . . . bathroom cupboard, I think," and he dashed upstairs.

"Madeleine! Marcus Aurelius!" called Roland. "Quick! Come and look! It's Magnus!"

Madeleine shot out of the sleeping compartment, Marcus limping hurriedly after her.

"Oh, no!" she wailed. "He's dead!"

"I think not, Maddie dear," said Marcus excitedly. "Observe his respiration!"

"His what?"

"He breathes," said Roland.

"Oh, my precious baby!" cried Madeleine, and she popped through the wire and scuttled across the table.

At that moment Jim's footsteps sounded on the stairs.

"Cave hominem!" called Roland urgently, and when Madeleine took no notice of the warning he gave a tremendous alarm-thump with his hind legs, a thump so loud and reverberating that it would have woken the dead. In fact, it woke the living.

"Mummy?" murmured Magnus dazedly and, "Mummy's here, my baby!" cried Madeleine, and into the kitchen came Jim, the smelling salts in his hand.

At the sight of an ordinary little brown house mouse on his kitchen table, a house mouse moreover with the cheek to sniff at his precious King, the ratcatcher reacted instinctively. Ordinary mice, like ordinary rats or any other kind of ordinary vermin, were, for him, creatures to be killed, without cruelty if possible but also without a second thought. He picked up a rolling pin from the counter.

Afterward neither Marcus Aurelius nor Roland could exactly remember what occurred in the next few seconds. Did Madeleine shoot underneath Magnus for protection? Or did he somehow rouse himself to cover her little body with his giant one before the threat of the upraised rolling pin?

But what neither Marcus Aurelius nor Roland could ever forget was what happened next. They saw Jim start his downward stroke and then, horrified, stop it. They saw Magnus rise to his feet upon the cushion, stiff-legged, his coat hair on end, his black eyes focused once more and snapping with fury. They waited for the old cry of "Nasty! Bite you!"

Instead, to their amazement, there burst from Magnus Powermouse a gush, a stream, a positive raging torrent of words.

"Now look here," he cried angrily, staring up at Jim the Rat. "Just what exactly do you think you're

doing? I don't pretend to understand what's been happening—last thing I remember was running along a road looking for my parents—can't think how they and Uncle Roland got here—but that's not the point. The point is that you were just about to hit my mother on the head. My mother! The dearest, kindest, sweetest, little old mother any mouse ever had! What's the idea—treating me like a king, giving me all that marvelous grub"—and he licked his lips even in the middle of his tirade—"and then you want to bash my old mother's brains out! If you ever try to do such a nasty thing again I shall, without the shadow or semblance of a doubt, that is to say, indubitably, bite you. Or my name's not Magnus Powermouse! Which it is."

He paused for breath. From under his bulk Madeleine crept, her mouth open, her eyes on stalks.

"You mark my words," said Magnus.

CHAPTER 16

A Good Square Meal

In stupefied silence they marked his words.

"Markie!" whispered Madeleine at last. "He's talking! Proper!"

"Proper*ly*."

"That's what I said. He's talking! How d'you suppose he done it?"

"*Did* it."

"What?"

"He *did* it, Maddie dear."

"Yes, I knows that, stupid, but how?"

Marcus Aurelius looked consideringly at his son, so newly talkative. Roland, experienced now in translating even the most ponderous speeches, moved closer to Madeleine.

"Upon reflection—" said Marcus Aurelius.

"Thinking about it," muttered Roland.

"—it is not without the bounds of probability—"

"Seems likely."

"—that the reason for the boy's loquacity—"

"Why Magnus is talking so much."

"—may relate to the recent misadventure—"

"Could have something to do with his accident."

"—in the course of which—"

"When."

"—he may have received a concussion—"

"He could have got a bang."

"—in the cranial area."

"On his head."

"Crumbs!" said Madeleine. "It loosened his tongue!"

All this time Jim the Rat had not moved except to lower the rolling pin in the face of the loud and obviously angry fusillade of squeaks from the King Mouse. Now suddenly he felt quite weak with shock at the thought that he had come close to inflicting terrible injury upon His Majesty—and for the second time that morning! He sank into a chair, unstoppered the bottle of smelling salts and took a sniff.

Once he had stopped choking, and had wiped his eyes with his large red white-spotted handkerchief, Jim could see that the little brown house mouse had been joined by another, a gray one with a crippled foot. The pair of them fussed and frolicked around the King Mouse with obvious joy and excitement, and suddenly Jim realized. "Of course!" he said softly. "It's your mum and dad!" He mopped his brow. "Whew!" he said. "I nearly bashed your old mother's brains out!"

Inside the hutch, Roland scrabbled eagerly at the wire netting, and Jim reached over and undid the catch of the door.

"I suppose you're his uncle," he said with a grin.

The big white lop-eared rabbit hopped forward to join the mice and a chorus of squeaks and grunts broke out.

"Oh, Uncle Roland!" cried Madeleine joyfully. "You said we'd all meet again! You said it, sure as I'm sat here!"

"Sure as I'm *sitting* here," said Marcus Aurelius.

"Oh, Markie, I just said that. Why, I can remember the very words you used. You could see it all in your mind's eye, you said—'the triumphant reunion of Magnus Powermouse—' "

" '—with his pretty little mother—' " put in Marcus.

" '—and his wise father,' " finished Madeleine.

"I did indeed," said Roland, and he could not keep a little note of pride from his voice, "and I am so happy for you all." He turned to Magnus. "Are you all right, my boy?" he asked.

"Yes, thanks, Uncle Roland," said Magnus. "Right at this moment there's only one thing I need and that's food. Watch this!" And he shouted at Jim his first and favorite word.

Obediently the ratcatcher produced a Smartie from his pocket. At the approach of his great hand Madeleine and Marcus Aurelius jumped nervously away.

"It's all right," said Jim. "Take it easy. I won't hurt you."

"It's all right," said Roland. "Take it easy. He won't hurt you."

"If you says so, Uncle Roland," said Madeleine tremblingly. "But I don't mind telling you I was so scared I nearly squeaked."

Marcus Aurelius giggled nervously. "It was a near squeak," he said.

Watching Magnus bolting his Smartie, Jim suddenly realized that in all the drama of the morning he had had no breakfast.

"What we all need," he said, "is a good square meal."

"What we all need," said Magnus, "is a good square meal."

Jim turned and made for the larder.

"I must say," said Roland, "you have him well trained."

Soon the ratcatcher was back with a tray, which he placed carefully before them. For Magnus of course there was a Mars Bar. Roland had a monster carrot. Before Madeleine and Marcus Aurelius, Jim placed a large hunk of Cheddar.

He watched them as they sat upright, the food held between forepaws, nibbling eagerly, their black eyes fixed on him. His Majesty's mum and dad, he thought. I'd love to know all about him right from the start. If only you could speak.

He grinned at them. "Hard cheese," he said. "It's only mousetrap."

"I think he's trying to tell us something," Madeleine said. "What's he saying, Magnus, d'you know?"

"I don't know, Mummy, I'm afraid," said Magnus. "That's all the noise humans can make, that rumbling sound. If only they could speak. Compared to animals, their ability to communicate seems rudimentary in the extreme."

"Magnus . . . Powermouse!"

"Mummy?"

"You're getting to talk just like your father!"

Marcus Aurelius looked smug through his mouthful of cheese. Roland's nose twitched madly.

"Well, anyways," said Madeleine, taking another bite, "I reckons we'm onto a good thing here. The man may not be able to speak proper, but he isn't going to let us go short. Look at him now!" For Jim, his own breakfast in the frying pan, was busy providing a further range of delicacies for his guests.

For the vegetarian Roland there were cabbage leaves, bread, an apple. And for the others biscuits, a handful of cornflakes, Smarties, bacon rinds.

"It's always like this," said Magnus, picking up a Petit Beurre. "He keeps a good table."

At last the feast was finished. Jim the Rat had pol-
ished off his favorite meal of bacon and eggs and
sausages, and bread and honey, and cups and cups of
sweet tea made with goat's milk. Roland lay happily
sated, his great ears outspread, his red eyes half-closed.
The little stomachs of Madeleine and Marcus Aurelius
were as round and tight as balloons. And even Magnus
had had enough.

"Crumbs!" said Madeleine. "I can't eat no more."

"I can't eat *any* more," said Marcus.

"Not surprised."

Marcus Aurelius cleared his throat importantly.

"I shall make a speech of thanks," he said. He turned
to face Jim.

"My good fellow," he began.

"Marcus . . . Aurelius!"

"Yes, Maddie?"

"You can't talk to a human like that."

Marcus Aurelius sighed. "My dear Maddie," he
said in a patient voice, "on the one hand there seems
no doubt that he *is* a good fellow, and on the other
he cannot understand what I am saying anyway."

"Then why bother to say it?" murmured Madeleine
comfortably.

Magnus intervened. "What you want to do," he
said, "is make a fuss of him. Humans like animals to
do that, you know, it makes them feel wanted. They're
ever so insecure. Go up to him. Let him stroke you."

"Stroke me?" cried Madeleine and Marcus Aurelius
together.

"Magnus is right," said Roland drowsily. "Just treat him kindly, and he'll be so grateful, you'll be eating out of his hand."

Marcus Aurelius looked nervously at the fat man who sat watching him with eyes the color of the bottom of a duck pond.

"I am apprehensive," said Marcus Aurelius in a low voice, "very apprehensive." He paused. "Very apprehensive indeed," he said.

"Well, I wish I was then," whispered Madeleine. "You're lucky. I'm just scared."

Marcus Aurelius looked at his misunderstanding little wife whose love he so valued, at the great white rabbit whose friendship he so esteemed, and at his giant son whose strength and courage he so much admired. He took a deep breath and squared his thin shoulders, and then he limped forward toward Jim the Rat.

And behind him, trembling but ever loyal, came Madeleine.

As Magnus and his Uncle Roland watched, Jim put out a hand to each, very slowly, and touched the gray back and the brown back, very softly, and stroked them, very gently, very tenderly.

"You know, Uncle Roland," said Magnus Powermouse, "I shouldn't be surprised if we didn't all live happily ever after."

CHAPTER 17

Tailpiece

And so they did.

Jim the Rat gave up rat catching. He offered his clients a variety of reasons for his retirement. "Getting near the pension anyway"—which was true, "The old van's on its last legs"—which was true, or "Just fancy staying at home all day"—which was also true. He gave no one the real reason, which was that he simply could not keep the King Mouse and his parents as pets, no, more than pets, as friends, and at the same time spend his life slaughtering their brothers and sisters and cousins.

Roland took up marriage. Jim just happened to come across such a pretty doe rabbit one market day—such a long soft coat she had, as blue as woodsmoke among the trees—and so the uncle of many nephews and nieces soon became the proud father of many sons and daughters; some were blue and some were white, some had prick ears and some had lop ears; all grew up happily with their dad's great friends, the giant mouse and his parents.

Madeleine and Marcus Aurelius lived a life of luxury. Jim built them a beautiful new house, a cage it was really but they never thought of it like that since they were always free to go out if they wished.

(Strangely enough, Jim's three cats never again came into the kitchen.) Once in a while, for old times' sake or if it was specially cold, they would spend a night with old Uncle Roland, warm under their velvety bedspreads. Fortunately, Jim gave them newspaper as nesting material so that Marcus always had plenty of interesting reading matter. Madeleine, relieved of the ceaseless search for food and the constant threat of danger that had been her lot, grew comfortably stout. Magnus, surprisingly, did not grow any more. Maybe it was that bang on the head or maybe he would have stopped anyway, but he became no bigger.

What he did become—and this must have been the bang—was extremely wordy. The newfound art of conversation became a great joy to him, and he and Marcus Aurelius would chatter away till all hours, putting the world to rights. Sometimes they would have an evening at Uncle Roland's house and his deep voice would be heard, trying to get a word in edge-ways.

And there was a time when Madeleine, sitting and listening to the ceaseless flow of talk, felt just a little bit left out; maybe because, as usual, she did not understand half of what they were saying; maybe because she was chewing on a pale-colored Smartie, which suddenly reminded her of a Pennyfeather's Patent Porker Pill and those long-ago days when Magnus was a baby and helpless and could not string two words together.

And suddenly Magnus realized that whatever adventures lay ahead for him (and many and exciting they were to be), yet somehow to his mother he would always remain a child. At that instant he knew exactly what she was feeling, and left the others, and came over to her, and gently touched her little nose with his big one.

"Nice Mummy!" said Magnus Powermouse softly.

"Oh, my baby!" said Madeleine. "There won't never be another like you."